SO-AZA-452

ALL I *REALLY* NEED TO KNOW I LEARNED IN PRIMARY

Discovering Life's Treasures

A NOVEL

Brenton G. Yorgason & Donald P. Mangum

Jacket art and sketches by Aaron Fairbanks Yorgason.

Jacket Design by Jim Knight Design, Provo, Utah.

Printed by Press America, American Fork, Utah.

© 1997 Brenton G. Yorgason and Donald P. Mangum

All rights reserved. No part of this book may be reproduced in any form
or by any means without permission in writing from the publisher,
Lighthouse Publishers, 291 West 4100 North, Provo, Utah, 84604. This
work is not an official publication of The Church of Jesus Christ of
Latter-day Saints. The views expressed herein are the responsibility of
the authors.

First printing August 1997

Library of Congress Cataloging-in-Publication Data

Yorgason, Brenton G., 1945-
    All I really need to know I learned in primary.

    I. Mangum, Donald P. II. Title.

ISBN 0-9659559-0-7

Printed in the United States of America
10 9 8 7 6 5 4 3 2 1

To our grandchildren, both present and future, who will hopefully fall heir to the whims of their two grandfathers--and receive childhood treasure chests of their own. After all, isn't that what grandfathers are for? We hope to spoil them royally. After all, it seems only fair that they have the same blessings of grandparenting--and the same treasure-filled boxes--that we had during *our* youth.

ACKNOWLEDGMENTS

We wish to thank our former Primary teachers, who taught us much more than we presently remember. A sincere thanks is also given to our former students, Primary and otherwise, who provided many encouraging suggestions. We make special note of Larry Gunther's contribution to this book. His ideas were instrumental in the development of the story.

In addition, we thank those who have read earlier versions of this manuscript, and who offered their perspective and suggestions. These include Tom and Cathy Pickren, Kay Schmalz, Leo and Shirley Weidner, Gladys Margetts, Mark Kastleman, Dan and Judy Bell, Dale and Shari Stone, Richard Smith, Andrew Allison, Jay and Joan Mitton, DeLynn and Melva Heaps, Teri and Dennis Crockett, Ron and Jan Johnson. We also thank our editors, Linda Martin and Louise Williams. Their assistance has been invaluable. Last, but really *first* we thank our wives, Margaret and Diane. Without their support and encouragement, as well as their endless late night critiques, this book could not have been written.

Lastly, we express appreciation to our parents for encouraging, and at times even *insisting* that we attend Primary. Hopefully, the fruits of their nudges are being passed to future generations even as we continue to write.

TABLE OF CONTENTS

PROLOGUE   1

1 *Boxed In*   3

2 *Uncle ValGene and the Swedish Temple*   11

3 *Decision, Indecision*   18

4 *If It's the Right Battle,*   21
   Don't Worry About the Scars

5 *The Rescue*   27

6 *That My Family Might Partake*   32

7 *Silence May Be Golden, But the Truth is Priceless*   34

8 *Into the Forbidden Past*   40

9 *A Girl Named Maria*   42

10 *The Cleansing*   44

11 *It's Not My Fault, It's In My Jeans*   48

12 *To Be Or Not To Be*   52

13 *Buddy Ramsey Meets Godzilla*   54

14 *To Become Acceptable*   60

15 *Of Boards, Nails, and Wrinkles* 64

16 *Another Difficult Call* 69

17 *Faith Works* 73

18 *Awkward Moments* 77

19 *Matchsticks & Mansions, From The Eyes of a Sloth* 80

20 *The Tide Begins to Turn* 88

21 *The Greatest Love of All* 92

22 *Paying the Price* 103

23 *What's An Older Brother For?* 107

24 *With Christ in the Picture* 111

25 *Though Your Sins be as Scarlet* 113

26 *The Olive Branch* 125

27 *They Shall Be White As Snow* 132

28 *Sharing Feelings* 136

EPILOGUE 147

*P*rologue
Late Summer Evening — The Mid 1950's

In a small central Utah town, an eight-year-old boy has just gone to bed. If we had looked in on him only moments before, we would have seen Richard "Ricky" Allred going through a routine that was known only to him. After changing into his pajamas, he knelt down by the side of his bed and pulled a well-crafted box from underneath. Retrieving a shiny, new, plastic rowboat from a night stand nearby, he returned to the box. Glancing down inside, he found a vacant compartment and carefully placed the boat into it.

After closing the lid of the chest and sliding it back under his bed, he walked across the room and turned out the light. Then he carefully walked back across the room to avoid stepping on his dog, Conrad, who was dozing nearby. Kneeling for a brief prayer, he hopped into bed and quickly fell asleep.

Two hours later, in another city less than three hundred miles away, a decidedly different scene was unfolding. Eight-year-old, raven-haired Maria Tierlink sat at the top of the stairs, watching and listening. Her cheeks were pushed up against the rails. While peering unnoticed at the scene below, tiny tears formed at the corners of her eyes, and she wasn't sure why. She had heard conversations of similar tone and content from her parents before, but somehow she knew this time it was different. Still, it would be some time before the full impact of this evening was *realized* in her life.

"Oh, William," the woman pleaded frantically, *"please* don't do this! I know there are problems, but we can work them *out!!"*

"It's no use, Enid," the man fumed. "I've tried now for years, and all I do is cause more pain! It will be better for everyone if I just get on with my life and let you get on with yours!"

Pacing the dining room floor, the man seethed with anger and frustration. Back and forth the conversation went with the woman pleading and the man resisting. After several heated exchanges, a final plea was made: "William, think about *Maria!* You know how much you love *her!* If not for me, then please stay for Maria!"

"We've been through this before, Enid. I've thought about it, and I'm certain Maria will be better off without me. I've made up my mind, and it's final! When I leave here tonight, the two of you will never be burdened by me again. Don't try to find me either, because it won't do you any good!"

Not fully comprehending what was happening, a frightened Maria watched her father walk across the threshold of the house for the last time. As he departed--in a tirade of frustration and anger--he reached back and pushed the door shut with all the force he could muster! It had begun—

1

*B*oxed In

The Mid 1990's — Upstate New York

Slam!!!

Standing alone in the suddenly darkened attic, I felt chills running up my spine. Instantly the hair raised on the back of my neck. I wished with all my heart that I had propped the door open and brought a flashlight into the attic with me. I had been afraid of the dark since I was a small boy in Utah. And now it was no different. I was in the attic for only the second time since we moved into our home six weeks ago. The single hanging light overhead didn't work, so throwing caution to the wind, I began stumbling over boxes through the blackness that engulfed me. I couldn't even see where the door was, let alone how to safely navigate the haphazardly strewn about boxes.

All at once I froze! The floor beneath me creaked, and suddenly I felt like I was *not* alone. As this thought entered my mind, I saw a slight glimmer of metal in front of me. Extending my hand toward the object, I immediately grasped the padlock of what had to be my childhood wooden chest. As both hands now examined the hinges and the lid, the most eerie sensation came over me. Unable to breathe, and unable to remove my hands from the box, I found myself mechanically lifting it into my arms. Then, hesitating only briefly, I walked gingerly toward the door.

Once there, I grasped the handle and managed to open the creaking oak door far enough to push my foot into the crack. Tightening my hold on the chest, I pulled the door open toward me. With some relief, I walked across the lighted hallway and went directly into my study. I placed the dusty chest on the table next to the window and collapsed into the recliner behind me. Perspiring profusely, I sighed audibly, caught my breath, and wiped my forehead again. I stared intently at the chest, wondering about the fear that still gripped my heart. It was at this instant, as my eyes were fixed on the treasure chest of my youth, that an unexpected calm swept over me every bit as measurable as the chills of fright I'd experienced only moments before.

"That's strange," I found myself saying out loud. "I haven't really thought of this chest in years. So what is possessing me now. . . ?" As my words pushed out into the stillness of the room, I found myself absently getting to my feet. Taking Lemon Pledge and a dust cloth from the hall closet, I began polishing the old box like it was the most important piece of furniture I owned--for so it seemed. Yet until this moment it had been nothing more than a piece of old furniture. Now, however, with an energy that I found surprising, I began polishing it until the wood grain, as well as the metal hinges and lock, were shiny and dust-free-- reviving the former beauty of the box.

Suddenly the phone rang, jarring me back to the present. Answering, I was surprised to be speaking to our ward executive secretary, Rod Stoneham. This call, along with my unnerving experience in the darkened attic, removed any semblance of serenity from my day.

I wasn't surprised, or even concerned, when Brother Stoneham asked if I would meet with the bishop the

4

following day, right after our meetings. But his second request did cause my anxiety to rise. He asked that I bring my wife Maria along, because the bishop had something very important to talk with us about. Somehow I knew my life was about to change significantly.

Within minutes following Brother Stoneham's call, I had an unexpectedly strong impression to move my childhood box, and place it on the side-table, facing into the room.

This is strange, I considered, again wiping my forehead on my sleeve. *I haven't thought of this box for years, and now someone . . . or something . . . is selecting a place for it in my study.*

Strange or not, I followed through with my impression. It seemed odd that I was suddenly so concerned about the box; although I did have to admit that it made a nice addition to my study--and furthermore, it allowed me to re-live that Christmas morning, almost a life time earlier, when I received it from my favorite uncle, ValGene Allred.

The following morning as we were preparing for Church, I told Maria of my experience of locating the box and of my concerns about the phone call from Brother Stoneham. I reminded her that my new job as assistant superintendent of schools would literally demand most of my time. Maria gently suggested that I just *might* be jumping the gun with my concerns.

"After all, Richard," she said with a sly wink, "maybe the bishop is going to ask you to serve as Primary pianist."

"You don't ask a man to bring his wife along if you're going to call him to serve as Primary pianist," I retorted, feeling somewhat impatient that she didn't seem to understand my growing sense of anxiety. The conversation ended abruptly, and within moments we were on our way to the chapel. As we drove along, I found my mind thinking about how our lives had changed since our recent move to sleepy Mendon, New York, from bustling New York City.

House hunting had been an adventure from beginning to end. My lifelong interest in historical treasures resulted in an overwhelming desire to acquire one of the many antique homes in the area. We eventually found the perfect five-bedroom home near the center of Mendon--the very home town of Brigham Young prior to his joining the Church--and within two weeks we were settled in.

And did our home ever qualify as an antique--over 150 years old with most of the original building structure intact! We instantly loved many things about it, but were particularly pleased with the pine floor boards, old doors with latches instead of modern doorknobs, and an open brick fireplace between the kitchen and the family room. However, the feature that was a continual bother to a man of six-foot-seven, like myself, was the low door frames made for men of another era. Several times in the few short weeks since we purchased our home--especially when preoccupied or in a hurry--I had come in contact with these doorways. Even so, this feature as well as the others simply added to the charm of the old, white clapboard house.

In the midst of my reverie, I realized that we had arrived at the chapel, and my daydreaming was immediately replaced by a growing anxiety about the upcoming interview. At the conclusion of the meetings, Bishop Wilsted warmly ushered us into his office. After visiting briefly, he called me to serve as the ward Young Men's president. Assuring me that the call came from Heavenly Father, he promised that I could count on the Lord's help. Still, I just couldn't feel much enthusiasm for such a time-consuming task. After all, there were 28 boys on the Aaronic Priesthood rolls, and many were from less-active or part-member families. How could I possibly meet this new challenge while fulfilling my duties at home and at work?

Although I had never turned a call down in my life, I found myself saying, "Bishop, with the demands of my new job, I just don't know how I can do this. Would you mind if I gave it some prayerful thought--at least for the rest of the afternoon?"

Maria was unusually quiet on the way home, but later in

the afternoon she reminded me of our agreement several years earlier to let the Lord decide when and where we would serve. "Well, that's good theory," I snapped, a little out of sorts, "but it's not so easy when the heat's on! How can I balance all of this--husband, father, new assistant school superintendent, and now Young Men's president?!"

After lunch I went upstairs to the study. While pondering this dilemma, I glanced across the desk, allowing my eyes to once again *fix* on my beautiful, old treasure chest. In a haunting way, I began mentally to rehearse its history. At first I just vividly remembered my Uncle ValGene handing the box to me on that Christmas morning long ago. At the same time he gave similar chests to my cousins, John and Sterling.

Then I could see the event in my mind's eye more clearly, like it was happening now. It all came back in an unexpected rush, and it seemed like I was actually *participating* in the events while they unfolded before me. Suddenly I could hear Uncle ValGene's familiar voice. "Now boys," his pleasant words rang out as he looked directly at us, "these boxes are your personal treasure chests."

The word *treasure* grabbed hold of our minds, and in seconds we quickly opened our boxes to see what treasures they contained. Almost simultaneously we looked up at Uncle ValGene with crestfallen faces.

Sterling was the first to speak. "What do you mean *treasure chests*? They're just empty boxes!"

Having obviously caught our attention, Uncle ValGene explained why he had built and given each of us a strange, empty box. "As you look inside these chests, boys, you will notice that they contain no treasures today--only sectioned areas in the bottom of the box where you may *store* your treasures. Over the coming years, I want you to place special mementoes in these compartments. Be on the lookout for reminders of special moments of learning so that you can keep forever the things of greatest value to you. I

7

promise you that as you do this, unexpected events will occur later in your life that will help you rediscover the childhood treasures you've kept."

We thanked him, of course, but at the time I really didn't understand what he was saying. Although we were very young when this event occurred, we heard Uncle ValGene and our parents retell the story so often that the details were embedded forever in our memories. So, perhaps that's why everything seemed so vivid when I looked at the treasure chest this day. In fact, a flood of additional memories came into my mind as I continued to look at and to feel the chest.

Time passed and with encouragement from Mom and Dad, I did begin saving things. For example, shortly after I received the box, I found three robin eggs cradled in a nest in the branch of an old apple tree. The eggs were a novelty, and I vividly recalled showing them to my friends. Still, they were of little value, and before long they decayed and became smelly. That was when my mother helped me clean the remnants of the eggs out of the bottom of the box.

Time again rushed by, and I soon found that the best things to keep in my box were items that would last and couldn't break. I also learned to be more private about what I put into it, because older brothers had a habit of *borrowing* things--and somehow whatever they borrowed never seemed to find its way back into the box.

For a long time this chest was the most important thing I owned, and I kept it under my bed, directly beneath my pillow. Gradually, however, as I grew into my teens, I apparently lost track of its purpose. In fact, the next scene that unfolded in my mind didn't take place until shortly after Maria and I were married. We had stopped by my parents' home to pick up some of my things to take to our first apartment in Cedar City, and my mother insisted that we take the box with us. The old wooden chest was well past a decade in age, but she had polished it until it looked almost new.

Taking this childhood memento along seemed a bit of a

bother at the time. I knew it didn't really contain anything of value, but I fondly remembered receiving it from Uncle ValGene, so that alone probably would have convinced me to take it. But I finally gave in because of Maria's encouragement--a decision she would live to regret.

I next recalled seeing the old chest sitting in our living room in Cedar City, where it served as a conversation piece. But when we graduated and moved away, we simply stored it with other odds and ends, and the box was "out of sight, out of mind" until this particular weekend in Mendon.

Suddenly, as quickly as it began, the sensation of tumbling through time and space stopped. Again I was aware of sitting comfortably in my den, gazing absently down at the padlocked box. Without thinking I leaned over, picked it up, and carried it to my easy chair. Just holding it brought another flood of memories. The box itself was a treasure since it was handcrafted by my Uncle ValGene, who was one of the kindest men I had ever known. The workmanship was exceptional. Having learned his trade from my gifted carpenter grandfather, Hyrum Allred, Uncle ValGene was a skilled artisan. Most things he made by hand rivaled anything sold in a store.

Holding the box in my lap, to my surprise I could once again see Uncle ValGene's weathered hands as he presented it to me. As a child, I had always marveled at his hands. By the time he gave me this gift, he must have been in his late sixties, and his hands were becoming wrinkled with age. When he touched me, his hands felt rough on the outside-- the kind of roughness that comes from years of physical labor and from making treasures for others. But I also knew that his hands were gentle on the inside--a gentleness I couldn't forget even to this day.

As I sat there examining the box, I could once again remember his additional instructions about what to put inside. "It would be good," he would say, "if you could keep things that will help you remember how to live your life. You know, how to treat others, what ideas are important, that sort of thing. . . ."

For the next few moments, while wistfully thinking about Uncle ValGene and the box, I lost track of the time. Suddenly my mind returned to the present, and as it did, I immediately remembered the call from Bishop Wilsted. Once again, I was filled with anxiety. With these troubling feelings working back and forth in my mind, I placed the box on the table in front of me and began to move my hands slowly across the smooth, natural wood surface. Instantly, events began to rush through my mind in such a realistic fashion that it seemed as though my adult life suddenly vanished, allowing me to fall back . . . and back . . . and back. . . .

2

U*ncle* ValGene

and the Swedish Temple

"Ricky, Ricky, wake up; it's almost five o'clock! Uncle ValGene will be here any minute, and you aren't even dressed!"

That's Grandma's voice, I thought, *but how can that be? Where am I? What a dream that was! Now where am I? At Grandma's house? My cousins, Sterling and John, are sleeping in the next room. But why? Oh, yes . . . it's the first morning of fishing season! It's the Opener, Uncle ValGene is due at any minute, and I'm not ready. Better get hopping!*

Generally, eight-year-olds don't need much time to prepare for the day, and on this morning I was no exception. Quickly I threw on my fishing clothes. I gathered my messy hair up under my baseball cap and was hopeful that I could get away without combing it. I knew Uncle ValGene would be here any minute, so my two cousins and I ran downstairs to the kitchen where my grandma had prepared a fisherman's feast. Her oatmeal cereal and semi-burnt toast *always* tasted best on the *Opener!* And on this morning it

11

was no different, except that I *did* have to remove my cap long enough to offer the blessing on the food.

Not far from my grandmother's home was one of the finest fishing streams in *all* of central Utah. The quality of fishing there was a well-kept secret, known only to local fisherman and their families, so I could never divulge its legends. It was frequently whispered that those who gave away the secrets of the stream were doomed to never again catch a fish from its shady, tree-lined banks.

It was *no* secret, however, that every stream had its best fishing hole--and with this stream it was no different. Its favored spot was called the Swedish Temple after an old dance hall that used to be located just up the road. This special fishing hole was an unusually deep area in the stream that was coincidentally shielded from the sun by a large cottonwood tree. Over the years I'd always been able to catch big fish there. These giant, foot-long trout would hide way down deep, coming out to feed only when they saw a large, juicy worm swimming nearby.

So it was with great anticipation that on this Opener my cousins and I inhaled our oatmeal, donned our baseball caps, and piled into the car with Uncle ValGene. It was still dark as he drove us the half dozen blocks from Grandma's house to the Swedish Temple. We were intent on being the first ones there so we could fish uninterrupted at the best hole. As it turned out, we *were* the first to arrive and immediately staked out the very best fishing spots.

After sitting in the shivering darkness for what seemed like forever, the light gradually peaked over the hills to the east, signaling that it was legal for us to drop our worm-filled hooks into the water. The time was 7:00 A.M. Somewhat impatiently, we had obeyed the rules, so we should have felt happy about that. We were too focused on getting started, though, to think about the moral value of our endurance. Hurrying, we each put a large, squirming worm onto our hooks, then slowly lowered our lines into the stream. A hard tug let me know that I had a big one on the other end, so I jerked with all the might an eight-year-old could muster. Within seconds, a twelve-inch rainbow trout broke the surface of the water, and I shrieked with excitement. Uncle ValGene stood quietly in the background, allowing me to struggle while my two cousins helped me bring this prize catch the three feet to the shore.

I immediately jerked the half-eaten worm and hook from the trout's throat, then slipped a notched piece of wood through its mouth and along the opening of the gill. This secured the fish so that it couldn't flop around and get free again. After putting fish and stick down into the water at the side of the stream, I quickly worked another worm onto my hook and slowly lowered it back into the stream. After all, I was having great luck, and I didn't want it to end. Although I was elated with my success, I knew that any loud noises would scare the fish away and spoil it for the others. So I sat quietly and let my bait sink to the bottom of the Swedish Temple.

At that instant, without looking over at me, Uncle ValGene gently whispered, "Now boys, I want you to promise me that you'll only keep fish that are of legal size-- those that are at least six inches long. Also, I want you to promise that you'll never catch more than your limit or more than you can eat. This little stream provides a lot of fish for people, and you should never take advantage of its generosity."

To be honest, I had never thought about considering others who were not there while I was fishing. It was a novel idea, but deeper than the Swedish Temple for an eight-year-old. Without considering his comments further, I went back to the business at hand. I just knew that there were many more of those prize fish waiting for my gigantic wiggly worms.

Not long after Uncle ValGene gave us his words of caution, he walked over to the huge cottonwood tree nearby and sat down. He didn't want to crowd us, however, so he inched his way around to the other side until I could no longer see him. Before long we simply forgot he was there, and we continued tempting those unseen trophies hiding in the depths of the fishing hole.

Probably thirty minutes passed, yet none of us had so much as another bite. Still, we fished in silence. We knew that this hole never really quit--it just *teased*. After all, fishing *was* an exercise in patience--a concept almost impossible for a boy my age to grasp. Soon two other boys arrived at the Swedish Temple. By the size of them, anyone could see that they were a year or two older than any of us; and this fact immediately struck fear into my heart. Besides, I knew one of them was Buddy Ramsey. He had terrorized kids in our town for years and seemed ready to do it again. My anxiety proved to be justified, too, as Buddy and his friend immediately began to swear and yell at us, demanding that we move on down the stream so they could fish at the Temple. "After all," Buddy boasted loudly, "we made dibs on this hole last night, so we have the right to fish here!"

I knew his claim was false, because my dad had told me that no one could claim sole possession of the Lord's creations. Adding insult to injury, though, Buddy's friend grabbed the fish I had caught and held it up. "This is *my* fish," he announced. "I saw it yesterday and laid claim to it then. So, now it's mine!"

What these bullies didn't know, of course--and what *I* had almost forgotten--was that Uncle ValGene was sitting quietly behind the big cottonwood with his back resting against it. After he had heard enough of their claims, he stood up and shuffled into view.

"Good morning, boys," he said pleasantly, tipping his wide-brim Stetson hat in their direction. "Now, if I were you, I would just put the fish back where you found it, then move on down the stream. There are plenty of fish for everyone, and as you can see, this area *is* occupied."

As he finished speaking, Uncle ValGene slowly sat down next to me and gazed into the water. His action left the intruders with no choice but to depart. I immediately got the feeling that he glanced down because he knew that this tactic would avoid further confrontation.

Those two bullies were taken by surprise for sure, so without saying another word they moved on down the stream to begin their fishing exploits elsewhere. After all, even though he was an older man, everyone knew not to mess with ValGene Allred. Besides, he was bigger than the two of them put together, so they really had no choice.

ValGene was my dad's oldest brother, and at the time he looked about a hundred years old to me. In reality, however, he was not quite seventy. Hard work had toughened him, so if he ever had to confront teenage boys, they knew to move on. *Everyone* knew ValGene Allred, and no one thought it wise to cross him. Truly, though, a kinder man I had never met.

After the older boys disappeared from view, Uncle ValGene made a gentle observation. "Kids," he began, while continuing to look down into the water, "you have just seen how *not* to behave. When you become angry and tell lies, and when you decide to *take* instead of *give*, you will never succeed. I hope you will always be kind to others and that you will always tell the truth. It's the only way you can be truly happy."

At that instant, a giant grin formed across his face. He reached down inside his knapsack and pulled out a huge package of pink and white frosted animal cookies. What a treat! We came from large families, and store-bought cookies were rarely seen around our homes, especially cookies with candied icing. It was hard enough for our folks to keep us all fed and clothed. Knowing these circumstances, Uncle ValGene always seemed to provide special goodies on our outings.

Opening the package, he poured some cookies into my free hand. My other hand was still clasped tightly to the fishing pole. As I gobbled down the cookies, I'm sure I must have thanked him. However, all I could think of was how much I loved the animal cookies covered with icing.

As I sat there on the bank of the stream, time seemed to rush ahead. I could see that from that day forward, the events of that Opener would help kindle my desire to do things for others. In fact, from this day forward, whenever the Primary music leader led us in a rousing chorus of *Give Said the Little Stream*, I thought of Uncle ValGene and the Swedish Temple.

Continuing these flashes of childhood memories, I could see several years pass. Suddenly it was the day after Uncle ValGene passed away. The chapel was filled for his funeral, and I suspect most of the town was there. I heard my father say afterward that over a thousand people came to pay their respects.

During the funeral service, the speakers pointed out that although Uncle ValGene was always active in the Church, he never held any high office. He wasn't a very good public *"talker,"* they said, but he *was* a good private *"doer."* For example, his biweekly trips to the Manti Temple--for over 35 years--were legendary. So were the 29 years he served as ward clerk.

One of the speakers at his funeral reminded us that Uncle ValGene always had time for children and widows. I guess the theme of his funeral centered on his lifetime of hard work--much of it for the benefit of others. It seemed like everyone had been touched by his moments of giving.

Next I could see vividly several trips home. Whenever I returned there, someone always seemed to mention Uncle ValGene and one of his acts of kindness. On more than one occasion, I'd meet someone younger than myself--someone who didn't know me--and so I'd introduce myself. When they'd hear the last name of Allred, they'd ask, "Are you related to *ValGene* Allred? He was quite a legend around here, you know."

While still in this state of gathering old memories, I recalled with clarity the morning Uncle ValGene died. It was apparent that the end was near, and my father and I, along with many others, were at his bedside. In a quiet way, Dad asked Uncle ValGene if he had any fears. You know, was he afraid that he might flunk his final exam? Although Uncle ValGene seemed to be growing weaker by the minute, he still grinned his familiar grin, then reassured us all by saying that he was simply at peace. He went on to explain that he was looking forward to seeing Aunt Flora and his baby daughter Elaine. Elaine was his youngest child who had died in a fire a half century earlier, when she was only two.

Then, with a wink, Uncle ValGene added, "I also hear there's a lot to do up there, and I'm ready to go to work! I've been lying here in this bed way too long. . . ."

With these words echoing softly into the room, Uncle ValGene slowly closed his eyes. He then took several short breaths, smiled briefly, and silently passed into the world of spirits. Although his family knew that he did indeed have much to do, it occurred to me, while I was somewhere in the space between past and present, that perhaps just once in a while--maybe even on the first Saturday morning in June--he might be allowed to take a brief rest . . . on the grass-covered banks of the stream at the Swedish Temple.

3

*D*ecision, *Indecision*

As the gentle childhood memories of my favorite uncle began to fade, I once again found myself inside my study, holding the newly restored treasure box in my lap. Without thinking about it further, I picked up the phone and called Bishop Wilsted. Identifying myself, I told him that I would be honored to serve as Young Men's president. I started to apologize for waiting so long to respond, but he wouldn't let me get into that. Instead, he said that he understood, but had been certain of the outcome. In fact, he reaffirmed his impressions that I was the person the Lord wanted for the job.

After we finished our conversation, I once again looked at the treasure chest sitting before me. Placing it back on the table in front of the window, I somehow sensed that it wouldn't be long before I would be back in my study examining its contents.

Three nights later I returned home from work in a very agitated state. I knew the kids and Maria would be able to feel the tension, even though I said a little prayer as I walked into the house. Being preoccupied with the events of the day, I forgot to bend over as I entered through the doorway, and I bumped my head on the doorframe. This only added to what was already a very bad day. Maria met me in the entryway and gently asked me how my day had gone. She could see the strain in my face and the way I was holding my head, so she already sensed the answer. Still, she was trying hard to give me support and understanding. What I did not know--nor *would not* know for some time-- was that it was *Maria* who needed the support and understanding. For now, however, I simply considered my own situation.

"Not well," I retorted gruffly. "I just don't know what I'm going to do. If I don't stand up to the school board Thursday night, we may lose the library expansion. They just don't get it; these days it seems that everything is seen as money and taxes. Some of those people have no vision of the future or concern for it!"

Rejoining softy, Maria asked, "Why don't you relax in your den for a few minutes? I'll call you when dinner is ready."

"But you don't understand!" I snapped, still out of sorts. "If I do stand up to them, I may get fired. I don't know all the politics here. I'm not even sure the superintendent will support me if the board tries to get rid of me. If I lose my job, it'll be almost impossible to explain a short employment period on my resume. I'm just not sure it's worth taking a stand this early in the game."

With more encouragement--and with two aspirin and a glass of water--I agreed to go up to my den and cool down before dinner. Maria knew my temperament and was trying to help balance our children's need to interact with their father with my occasional mercurial disposition.

While waiting for supper, I sat behind my desk considering the pros and cons of the issues before the school board. Superintendent Ben Wilson was an excellent administrator and seemed to have confidence in me. It was his reputation, in fact, that had led me to accept employment in upstate New York in the first place. I should add that he *had* told me I should look at the issues regarding the library expansion, and he would support my choice. However, as yet we hadn't crossed the Rubicon together, and I wasn't sure he would really back me if I *did* take a strong stand.

As I sat pondering the best way to tackle this problem, my eyes drifted around the room and settled on my treasure box. Half kidding, I said, "I wonder if I could get that old box open. . . ."

Standing up, I walked over to the table, picked up the chest and placed it on my desk. For some reason I still hadn't opened it since I brought it down from the attic, so retrieving a large screw driver from the desk drawer, I began to force open the rusty keyless lock. When it finally broke, I slid the screw driver between the lid and the base, and the lid creaked open. There inside the box, protected from any intrusion for longer than I could remember, were numerous remnants of my past. In a way, I felt like I was looking down into a time tunnel that connected the present to my almost forgotten past. Little did I know, at that moment, how real these feelings would become.

Some of the items had been jostled out of their compartments, so I carefully moved things around until all seemed in order. Coming into physical contact with some of those mementoes--most all of them from my Primary days-- created spine-tingling sensations. It eerily seemed as though I were reliving some of the events associated with each object.

I quickly shook off these impressions, however, and began to examine one of the mementoes inside the box. There, as if it had been placed in it only the day before, was a forest green piece of felt. I picked it up and ran my hands across the material . . . then slowly I began to see images. At first these images were in the far distance, but then they came closer and closer until. . . .

4

If It's the Right Battle,
Don't Worry About the Scars

Startled back to reality, I suddenly realized that everyone in Primary was singing except me. *Wow!* I thought. *That was some daydream!* It was so realistic that I somehow expected to actually be somewhere else. But, no such luck. By quickly glancing around, I could see that I was there in Primary, and instantly the difficulty of my present situation came back to me.

Looking down at my trousers, I remembered why I had tuned out the present in the first place. *I can't even enjoy this song,* I fumed. *All I can think about is the boys on my row wearing Levis, while I have to wear Sunday pants!*

It was a beautiful fall afternoon, and I was about to receive my very own forest green bandalo, the symbol of transition into the Trail Blazer classes for nine-year-old Primary boys. Because of the occasion, my mom had insisted that I wear Sunday pants. Moving into the Trail Blazer classes was a rite of passage that included the boys being separated from the girls. For me, getting away from girls was relief mixed with disappointment.

The bandalo was made from a piece of heavy green felt that lay across the shoulder and formed a "V" at the third shirt button. The bandalos made the boys look very grown up, so I could hardly wait to get mine. The girls also received a turquoise bandalo on the same day. But I liked ours best, and I was pleased that there was a different color for boys.

Earlier that day, I had hurried home from school and reluctantly changed into my Sunday pants. Then I rushed along to Primary, filled with anticipation and excitement. After all, going to Primary *did* have its benefits, since my older brothers--both Primary graduates--had to stick around the house and do the chores.

Opening Exercises soon began and when my name was called to come to the front of the chapel and receive the bandalo, I could hardly breathe. I looked up and saw the Primary president standing near the podium. I loved our Primary president, and I was proud of her. But you would expect that. After all, she *was* my mother!

Having my very own bandalo around my neck reminded me that it was actually made to carry achievement emblems. But the ceremony for nine-year-olds didn't include receiving a bandalo covered with the plastic tokens of previous Primary activities. Rather, we received an empty bandalo with only the plastic pine tree placed exactly in the center of the "V" at the bottom. The tree was a symbol of our being advanced into the Trail Blazer classes for our last three years of Primary.

I knew then that for the next three years, my classmates and I would spend many of our Primary days, as well as some time at home, working on projects that would allow us to receive additional plastic emblems to attach to our bandalos. I had always been most impressed with the one of the Salt Lake Temple, where Mom and Dad had been married. Thankfully, I didn't need to be married to earn the emblem, just do some genealogy stuff and go to the Manti

Temple to do baptisms for the dead. In those days, we could do baptisms for the dead *before* we turned twelve.

Before I left for school that day, Mom had reminded me that I would be receiving my bandalo that afternoon. Because of this, she had insisted that I wear my Sunday pants. I wasn't happy about that, because I didn't want to look different from the other guys. "They'll be wearing Levis," I protested, "and some of them will be receiving *their* bandalos!"

My argument fell on deaf ears, however. And, as a matter of emphasis, Mom restated one of her oft repeated family axioms: We Allreds never just follow the crowd. We don't *do* things because others do them. We make the right choices then quietly hope others will follow us. If we have to, we go it alone.

Good logic; tough application. It still left me as the only boy in Sunday pants that day at Primary. The guys weren't as hard on me as I anticipated though. And besides, they knew that my other pair of pants--my Levis--was just like the ones they were wearing.

In any event, there I was, standing in a row with the other kids my age, wearing my brand new Trail Blazer bandalo. And do you know what? I found myself thinking that I was the best dressed boy on the stand. Sometimes mothers just know what's up.

The girls, who were called Homebuilders, were also standing there--only they were wearing their bright turquoise bandalos. No Sunday pants for them, however, as they were all wearing their finest dresses.

The best part of that Primary day came later when some of the older girls approached me after the ceremony and told me how nice I looked. Of course, I pretended it didn't matter, but I couldn't help noticing that the other boys seemed a little jealous. Like I said, my mom really *did* know what was up.

Following those memorable moments, the rest of the day went pretty well--that is, until I was playing football on the church lawn after Primary. I was being very careful not to get too many grass stains on my Sunday pants. My team was winning by a large margin when Buddy Ramsey and several of his minions came along and decided to take over the game. They acted just as they had at the Swedish Temple. They told us that they claimed the field, and because they were older, they deserved to keep the football that actually belonged to Kent Gowers. Well, even though I was only nine, and quite a bit smaller than this group of bullies, I just couldn't let them get away with *that!*

"Come on, you guys," I blurted out, hardly knowing what I was saying, "this isn't *fair!* And I'm not going to let you do it."

"Hey, listen to Squirt here," Buddy taunted. "Who said anything about fair? Life isn't fair, Squirt, and not you or anyone else is going to stop us!"

Undaunted, I grabbed Kent's football right out of Buddy's hands and started to run toward my house. But I wasn't looking clearly, and I ran smack-dab into one of Buddy's friends. That mistake allowed just enough time for Buddy to catch up.

Leering down at me, Buddy saw my bandalo, which was still wrapped around my neck. In a flash, and before I could react, he grabbed the bandalo and jerked it hard. It tore right in half, and suddenly it was no longer around my neck. Instead, it was in Buddy's hand. He smirked a satisfying smirk, then threw it on the ground at my feet.

"Take that, Squirt!" he laughed tauntingly. Then, noticing some adult Primary leaders approaching, he added, "Come on, guys; we can find another football and another place." With that, he and his friends quickly left the playing field and headed toward town. It shouldn't have surprised us when they quickly vanished. Most everyone knows that bullies never stick around when the sides even up.

As they walked away, I reached down and picked up my bandalo. There was a rip right across the bottom that simply devastated me. I could hardly believe my misfortune. Nor could I imagine how I might be punished for allowing such a thing to happen.

Good fortune was on my side, however; I could see my mother among those coming across the field. She was carrying her Primary box, and she looked pretty cheerful. "Ricky," she called, "would you please carry this box home for me?"

Now we lived a full two blocks from the chapel, but I had recently developed quite a few muscles, so I knew my job would be easy. And with a little luck, maybe Mom wouldn't even notice the bandalo. So I quickly stuffed it into my back pants pocket, then held out my hands. She casually handed me the box and immediately swept her arm behind my back. When it reappeared, sure enough--there in her hand was my torn bandalo. By some magic, I had been caught dead-to-rights, and suddenly I knew there was no way out but to explain what had happened. As for Mom's face? Well, you'll not be surprised to know that her cheerful look all but disappeared.

"I...I'm sorry, Mom," I blurted. "I'll never do that again. It's just that . . . well, Buddy and his friends were making trouble. They wanted to take over the field and the game. What was I to do, just sit there and let them get away with it?"

Now my mother didn't know much about the rules of football, *or how bullies worked*; but she *did* know how *I* worked. So, allowing her pleasant disposition to return, she said, "Well . . . that's okay, because I'll sew it up for you the minute we get home. I have some matching green thread, and no one will know the difference. In fact, Ricky, this will now be a special bandalo. Only *you* will have one like it. All the others will look the same. But yours? Well, it will have 'battle scars.' Then whenever you wear it, you'll be reminded of this important day when you stood up for what you believed, even though it was very difficult."

With that pronouncement, Mom put her arm around me, and the two of us walked silently down the gravel street

25

toward home. I was glad she didn't give me a speech about acting foolishly, or mete out some kind of punishment. Instead, she allowed me to think on the matter and to consider how lucky I was to have a bandalo with battle scars. Trust my mom--who knew nothing about bullies, and even less about football--to turn my torn bandalo into something special.

The following Wednesday, as I entered Primary wearing my stitched-up bandalo, one of the teachers offered to get me a new one. But I knew that wearing mine was a privilege. So, smiling proudly, I calmly replied, "No thanks. This bandalo is something special. As you can see, it has battle scars."

With that I moved quickly into the row where my class was sitting and joined with them in singing the opening song. Was it just me, I thought, or was everyone admiring my unusual bandalo? This was a real treasure, and I knew where I was going to keep it forever and ever. What's more, I knew my mother had been right in what she had told me as we were walking to Primary. Her words, spoken with an energy that I could still feel, were simply this: *"If it's the right battle, Ricky, don't worry about the scars."*

5

*T*he Rescue

Blinking several times, I realized that I wasn't really in a Primary opening exercise at all. I was sitting in my den, my worn out bandalo in my hands. What's more, I was facing the challenge of a library expansion and an unsympathetic school board. Now, because of what I had learned so many years earlier, I knew what I had to do. I knew it *was* the right battle, so the scars would be justified.

Weeks passed. I can't say that I escaped from those library expansion discussions at the school board meetings *without* a scar, for I didn't. But I *can* say that the Darrell T. Thompson wing of the High School Library is well underway. Darrell Thompson, president of the school board and prominent citizen, initially opposed the addition to the library for economic reasons. However, perhaps the sound of the "Darrell T. Thompson wing" may have altered his perspective just a little. I guess even adults need symbols on their bandalos to help them understand the significance of the good they are doing.

I haven't had any direct encounters with my magical treasure box since the episode with the school board. Even so, there have been some rather unusual moments that bear repeating. After a relatively calm resolution of the library question, I chose not to tell Maria much detail of my experiences with the box, and I hadn't mentioned it at all to the children. However, on one occasion my unfortunate lack of forthrightness almost proved my undoing.

Not long after the library dispute, I came home from work and, feeling rather tired, went immediately to my study. Collapsing into my favorite chair, I turned on the stereo, closed my eyes, then started to drift off. In so doing, I reached my hand out to touch my treasure chest. Instead of touching it, however, I found my hand resting on an empty table--the table where the box normally sat. I was startled to say the least--simply because the box had always been there. Opening my eyes, I quickly glanced around the room, searching. Still, my old chest was nowhere in sight. Sensing that something was extremely amiss, I ran frantically down the stairs and found Maria. "Have you seen my treasure box?!" I pressed with noticeable irritation.

"Of course, Honey," she replied rather sullenly. "I've seen it every time I've dusted in your study. I also know that you haven't opened it in years, so I gave it to Tami Peterson today for the Boy Scout auction. You kept it in storage for so long that I knew you wouldn't mind. Besides, I found a bronze statue of an old pioneer couple down at the antique store. Knowing how much you love history, I thought you'd like *it* better than that old box. As soon as I clean the statue, I'll put it up on your table."

Too stunned to reply, I just stood there. I honestly couldn't believe what I was hearing. "I thought someone at the auction might actually like your old box," she continued, her voice tightening. "As they say, 'One man's trash is another man's treasure.'"

Maria finished her spiel with a surprising tone of

satisfaction that she had once-and-for-all solved a family *problem.* Her unusually energized explanation caused a feeling of panic to swell within me. *Why hadn't I told Maria details about my experiences with the treasure chest? More importantly,* I thought, *something is going on inside of her and she's not telling the whole story.*

"Maria," I stammered, pushing my analytical nature on the back burner, "we *must* get that box back! There is something happening with it that I can't even begin to understand. But we don't have time to talk about that now. How can I get it back?"

"Well . . . it will be embarrassing," Maria began with obvious reluctance, "but if I have to, I guess I can give Tami a call. The auction is not until tonight, so she may still have it."

After several unsuccessful phone calls that consumed the next two hours, Maria determined that our only hope was to attend the auction and make a bid ourselves. Needless to say, I wasn't too happy about that, but off to the auction we went. After posting a bid of $150, I was once again the relieved owner of my treasure chest. The bidding wouldn't have been so high, but the auctioneer couldn't get the box open. Then, when *I* started bidding, someone suggested that it must contain a valuable heirloom or something. Only Maria's resistance to such a notion caused the bidding to calm down before it got out of hand. As it was, we escaped with only minimal damage. I guess that a $150 contribution to a worthy cause was a small price to pay for having my chest back!

On our way home from the auction, I decided not to press Maria about giving away the chest. I wanted to, but something inside me told me to let it go, and so I did. What I *did* tell Maria were the details of my two prior episodes with the box. While she acknowledged that the incidents were a little baffling, she reasoned that coincidence alone might explain away the sense of time travel. She asked me if I were really outside of myself and watching these experiences, or if the memories were just very vivid. I explained that it was the latter, since I had truly seen the events of my past in vivid and long-forgotten detail. Then she raised what I thought was a peculiar question, as she asked if it were really that vital for me to reach back into my childhood.

Not comfortable with the way the discussion was unfolding and with how I was having to defend my recent experiences, I refocused the discussion on the chest, "Maybe just touching the box, smelling its old smells, and holding my Primary bandalo brought all those memories back to me. I think it's more than coincidence that I've found this gateway to my past. Let's have a Family Home Evening about it, and I can share some of my experiences with you and the kids. . . ."

"Let's *not!*"

Maria's words shot like lightning toward me. *What on earth's happening? Maria's got something on her chest, and she's not coming clean with what it is.*

Clearing my mind, I determined to deal with my feelings of betrayal. I would approach her unexpected anger from the back door and see where the conversation led. "Maria," I began slowly, "have I done something to upset you? I mean, is there any other reason that might have triggered your giving the box away?"

For what seemed like an eternity, but which was only two or three minutes, Maria said nothing. When she finally did reply, her words seemed oddly hollow. "I'm sorry, Richard. I'm just under a lot of pressure, that's all. Of course we'll have Family Home Evening, and of course the kids will enjoy whatever you might share with them. . . ."

Suddenly feeling Maria's fingers intertwine with my own, while she gazed silently out into the darkness of the night, I somehow sensed her need for privacy--and for acceptance. Something *was* bothering her, and although my childhood treasure chest was likely not related, somehow it seemed to have triggered her decision to give it away. Even so, now

30

was not the time to pry further, but to simply allow the moment to pass. And this is exactly what I did.

6

That My Family Might Partake

Not long after supper the following Monday evening, we gathered our entire family into my study. Many people have said our five children looked almost like stair steps because their ages were so evenly spread out over a ten-year period. Walter, named after my grandfather, and the oldest of our children, was now twelve. Sarah had just passed her tenth birthday. Luke, our musician, was almost eight, and Elizabeth was going on six. Our baby, Eve, broke the chain in two ways. She was only six months old, and the pattern of boy-girl, boy-girl was no longer intact.

Following a typically lengthy opening prayer offered by Luke, our aspiring patriarch, I placed the treasure chest on the floor before us. Relating some of the box's history, I told the children about Uncle ValGene's counsel and encouragement as he presented it to me. I further explained how I had spent some time learning how to select the best items *for* the box. They asked me about what I had chosen, and once again I had to admit that I really hadn't thought much about the contents since my childhood. But, I assured them, I was beginning to value their importance in my life. This allowed me to share the mysterious occurrences that took place when I wrestled with specific current problems, and how holding the box and the bandalo had led me to make a good decision.

Immediately Sarah caught on. "Dad," she pressed, "why don't you open up your chest and pick out something you think we might want to hear about?"

I have to admit that hearing Sarah make her request that way caused me to feel a little odd, simply because I couldn't tell if she were being sarcastic. But I agreed, and after some effort I pried the padlock open. As I did, I told the kids I would not allow them to see inside the box at this time--but that I would retrieve whatever item I felt inclined to. Naturally, the room was filled with groans, but I was resolute and they knew it, so they held back while I lifted the lid and peered inside.

Glancing over the partitioned sections of the chest, my eyes came to rest on an old wallet. As I picked it up, a sheepish grin spread across my face. This was a natural reaction to remembering one of those long-forgotten episodes that came from another lifetime. Gradually, the memories of the wallet and how it came into my possession began to flood my mind in vivid detail.

I picked the wallet up carefully and placed it in my lap. Then I began to share the story of the wallet's origin. As I proceeded, the narrative was accompanied with hauntingly *real* mental images. Although, strangely, Maria appeared to be resting with her eyes closed, I glanced at the kids and it was obvious that they were having an experience similar to my own . . . and the distance between past and present seemed to disappear for each of us.

7

Silence May Be Golden,
But the Truth Is Priceless

It must have been a short night, because I dozed off right during the closing prayer of Primary class. But gathering myself together, I said goodbye to my teacher, Sister Nofsinger, and started for the door. It surely wasn't today's lesson on honesty that put me to sleep, because I had really listened to the details. I guess my attentiveness was driven by two feelings, the first of which was guilt. After all, doesn't every young boy wince at one or two of the examples used in a lesson on honesty? The other feeling was probably a bit unrighteous, as I was looking for any angles on how to live the principle of honesty on the edge. Sister Nofsinger didn't leave any room for doubt, however.

After a quick summary of the lesson, she called on someone to pray. I think it was Darrell Fjel. It was then that I dozed off, right during his prayer. After rubbing my eyes awake, I stumbled out of the classroom. I must have still been daydreaming when I absentmindedly took the shortcut

34

through the woods between our house and the chapel. Usually I only took that route when I was with one of my classmates, but on this particular day I was walking alone. I don't remember *why* I was alone, and not being trailed by my dog, Conrad. At any rate, I wasn't really thinking about which way to go home as I entered the woods.

As I mentioned, the subject that day was *honesty*. This was a tough subject because it hit me where I was actually living. Honesty, of course, is never taught as an idea lesson. It's always taught as a "to do" lesson. The types of questions asked during a lesson on honesty are always the same. "Class, what would you do if . . . ?" Such lessons then seem to conclude with the one issue that is challenging those in attendance. And, if that isn't bad enough, the teacher then singles someone out to answer that specific question. It's easy to fake the answer, as if it were no problem to try *always* to make the right choice. Even so, on the way home, somehow such a response usually comes back to haunt you.

Well, anyway, that's what happened to me on this very day. We were taught a very good lesson on honesty; I had survived it, and now I was on my way home. As I walked deeper into the woods, I began to question myself about why I was in there alone. *What was I thinking about?* I wondered. I surely wasn't thinking about my secret girl friend, Maria. After all, she and her family had moved away the year before. At the time of her move, I considered hiding out among the boxes on the moving truck, but thought better of it because I hadn't even spoken to her. Nor had I to this day. It was just one of life's regrets and also one of *my* secrets.

Lost in thought, while walking deeper and deeper into the wooded forest, I almost didn't even see the increasing darkness. When I suddenly began to realize where I was and that I was alone, I became edgy--even frightened. There was still some daylight, and I could almost see my house, but everyone knew about the rumors. The older guys in our neighborhood told very detailed stories about a boy who, a few years earlier, entered the forest alone, never to be seen again on this planet. They never mentioned what planet he was seen on, and I didn't want to ask. Still, I _did_ think about it. . .

I was halfway through the forest when suddenly I spied a dark, wallet-size lump on the trail. As I approached it, my first impression was confirmed. It _was_ a wallet. I looked around very carefully, concerned that I was being watched, and I wondered if maybe this were a trap recently set by an alien force who had come back for _another_ little boy!

After glancing in every possible direction, I stepped closer to the wallet, anticipating that any minute I would drop into a trap or be pulled from the earth by an anti-gravity machine. Throwing caution to the wind, I suddenly lunged forward, grabbed the wallet, and jumped while gritting my teeth and expecting to be caught or destroyed by the space aliens.

Remarkably, I had avoided detection. I decided to open the wallet, but I knew that with _my_ luck it would contain alien money, and there was no way I could ever cash it in. I was wrong again--about the kind of money, I mean. Inside that wallet was $28.38. My heart seemed to leap into my throat as I quickly counted it, because that was about as much money as I had ever seen in one place. It was a literal fortune to a boy who paid only 14 cents to get into a movie!

I couldn't spend too much time thinking about the money, however, because as you know, I was standing alone in a dark forest while my life was hanging by a thread. _All of this might be a trick_, I considered quickly. _I need to get out of here before I'm vaporized_!

Glancing around, while looking for any sign of visitors from outer space, I noticed some scraps of paper several feet from where the wallet had been lying. Not fooled by this attempt to get me to stay longer, I quickly ran to the trail that led out of the woods. Within minutes I was in a clearing, my heart pounding so hard I thought it was going to explode. *But,* I thought, *if I can survive the next few minutes I'll be rich! And, if I can just make it across my yard without being lifted up to an alien vessel, I will actually live to spend my new-found wealth.*

Emerging from the woods, I stopped at the edge of my yard to catch my breath. Then I realized what was going to happen next: *as soon as I walk through the kitchen door, I will have to explain the wallet to my mother. If that happens, the wallet will vaporize for sure. Hum . . .* I considered thoughtfully, *maybe she's not home. Maybe she's out running errands, or something.* I looked toward the house, and my hopes were quickly vaporized--for I could see her through the kitchen window, fixing dinner.

Immediately, I began to form 'Plan B.' I quickly reviewed the situation and remembered an old saying I had heard. *Silence is golden.* Right then I discovered its *true* meaning--*golden,* as in getting rich. Thinking out my plan, I decided that I'd just sneak in the back door, go straight to my room, and hide the wallet in my drawer. That way, Mom would never know about it.

Not forgetting the immediate peril lurking somewhere around me, I ran quickly to the back door. Drawing a deep breath, I sauntered nonchalantly into the house. Mom immediately looked up from her dinner preparations and noticed me sliding along the wall. In a calm but penetrating voice, she greeted me with, "Hi, Ricky. What did you find in the woods?"

Is X-ray vision standard issue for mothers? Hoping with all my heart that I was wrong, I slowly replied, "Uh . . . nothing . . . nothing at all. But I sure had a great day at Primary!"

"Oh, that's right . . . today *was* Primary day," she responded with a voice that would freeze an alien stone cold. "What was the lesson about?"

Yikes, she had me! "Uh . . . it was all about . . . honesty, Mom," I answered slowly, while reaching into my front Levis pocket and pulling out the wallet. I had no sooner said "honesty" than I found myself unexplainably extending my arms toward my mother with the wallet clutched in both hands.

"Why, where did you find *this*, Ricky?" she asked innocently.

"In the forest," I confessed, with all the excitement of a condemned criminal.

Smiling gently, she pressed a little harder, "Whose wallet do you think it is, Ricky?"

Now I knew I was in for one of those dreaded teaching moments, because in every sentence Mom had said my name. Nevertheless, seeing a possible glimmer of hope, I replied, "Why, it's mine. I not only found it, but I risked life and limb to save it from alien forces. . . ."

"Is there any identification in it, Richard?" I was again troubled by the continued use of my name--my *formal* name--but I still held out hope for some chance of victory.

"Not a bit!" I replied triumphantly. "Why would an alien leave identification?"

"Richard," (there it was again . . . my *name*) "why don't we go back into the woods and see if we can figure out who this wallet belongs to?"

"That could be pretty risky," I countered, hoping to put a little anxiety into the mix. "The forest can be a very dangerous place you know, with the stories about aliens and all."

"Ricky, I've never heard of anyone getting nabbed in the woods if they traveled with someone older and bigger. So, let's you and I go together, okay?"

In what seemed like a matter of minutes, I was standing on the doorstep of Brother and Sister Parker's home, right down the street. Just as Mom had guessed, when we arrived back in the woods, we found some identification papers. They appeared to be the same papers I had seen earlier, but had mysteriously changed into an earthly driver's license and some other things, all with Brother Parker's name on them. I have to admit that it did make me wonder about *his* origins.

After I rang the doorbell, Brother Parker appeared. For a second I stared at him trying to sense any hint of alien appearance. I think he wondered what I was looking at, because after a few silent moments, he said, "Ricky, are you all right? Is there something wrong?"

Well of course, I couldn't tell him about my *real* concerns, so I gave a brief explanation about finding his billfold, then handed it to him. Opening it up, he pulled out all of the bills and fanned them out in front of me. For a moment I felt a surge of excitement--that is, until his fingers closed on a one-dollar bill which he offered to me.

At that instant, I remembered the day's Primary lesson about honesty. One of Sister Nofsinger's points was about returning things without thought of reward. Still I surprised myself when I said, "No, Brother Parker, it wouldn't be right. Uh . . . thanks, anyway. . . ."

Pushing the idea harder, while emptying out his wallet, Brother Parker added, "Well, Ricky, I have been going to throw this wallet away anyway. Would it be okay to give it to you?"

"Oh, if it's just going to be trash anyway, I guess I could take it," I responded with more than a small amount of excitement.

Looking back, I have to admit that as I walked home I truly *did* feel warm inside. I learned the value of the saying, *While silence may be golden, the truth is priceless.* Even so, I couldn't help wondering whether Brother Parker had any association with alien forces and the abduction I had heard so much about. After all, he *was* pretty strange looking.

That night before falling to sleep, I took the precautions any right-thinking boy would take under similar circumstances. Hiding the wallet in my treasure chest, I carefully bolted the door to my bedroom, made sure the window was locked tightly and the curtains pulled closed. Immediately I jumped into bed and pulled the covers over my head.

8

*I*nto the Forbidden Past

"Gee, Dad," Walter exclaimed with his typical enthusiasm, "that was *great!* How were you able to do that . . . I mean, get the story to come *alive?* Somehow it seemed like I was really *there!*"

"Tell us exactly what you saw, Walter. . . ."

Speaking hesitantly, he began. "Oh, I don't know. It wasn't exactly like a movie, or a dream, just somewhere in between. I mean, I could really see images just like you were describing. And sometimes I thought your voice faded out, and I could hear the voices of the people you were talking about. . . ."

As the others chorused similar impressions, I was even more puzzled by the strange occurrences associated with this wonderful old box. This was *remarkable!* They all seemed to accept the effects of my storytelling in a matter-of-fact way. For instance, when Elizabeth begged for one more story, the others encouraged me as well. Glancing over at Maria, I could see that she was again awake and involved, although she remained very quiet and seemed a little nervous. She didn't say anything, so I continued.

Lifting the top off the box and reaching inside, I retrieved an old Primary photograph--the one with me and my cousin Sterling in it. In fact, it was of my entire Primary class and was taken about the time I was five. It was rolled up like a scroll and was kept tight with a narrow ribbon tied around it. I wanted to examine it closely, so I picked it up and began staring at it. Then, predictably yet quite unexpectedly, I began to recall an event that transpired a very long time ago.

Unrolling the cracking photograph so the others could see, I again started a process that was growing strangely familiar. As I held the picture in my outstretched hands, I could feel myself slipping into a state that oddly felt like everything around me was fading from view. What's more, my voice sounded like I was in a long, long tunnel.

9

A Girl Named Maria

Five-year-olds live continuously on the edge of fantasy and reality, so I was not surprised to feel a sheepish grin creep across my face as I was walking home from Primary that afternoon. On that very day I had met the cutest girl I had ever seen. She had just recently moved in, and this was her first day in Primary. I noticed her right away and listened carefully as she was introduced.

"This is Maria," our teacher, Sister Newren, announced. "She will be a permanent member of our class."

The phrase "permanent member of our class" had a way of gripping my heart. I think I must have stared at Maria nonstop the entire class period--but still I couldn't bring myself to say anything to her after the closing prayer. I just continued staring as she left the room. Then I followed her down the hall at a safe and undetected distance until she disappeared out the front door.

Moments later when I arrived home, I was still thinking about Maria. I must have had that silly grin on my face-- because Mom stopped me and asked what was going on.

"Nothing," I lied.

"Why, Ricky, are you in love?"

Now, how my mother ever figured *that* out, I'll never know. Surprised by her reaction, I simply answered, "Well, maybe. . . ."

"What's her name, Ricky?" she slowly asked, a slight grin appearing on *her* face.

"Uh, why it . . . it's . . . Maria . . ." I stammered.

"Maria *what*?" she asked, not giving up.

I was stumped. I hadn't heard anything but "Maria," so I confidently announced that she didn't have a last name.

Mom's response was equally confident, as she said, "Ricky, I am sure that she has a last name. Perhaps next week you'll find out what it is."

She was right, of course. The next Wednesday I asked Sister Newren if she knew Maria's last name.

"It's Tierlink, Ricky. Why do you ask?"

Thinking quickly, I replied, "Oh, my mother wanted to know. . . ." And we left it at that.

After Primary I went home and acknowledged to my mom that she was right; Maria *did* have a last name; it was Tierlink. After that, I thought my mom was pretty smart. Why, she knew that Maria had a last name--and she didn't even know Maria.

10

*T*he Cleansing

"Daddy!" Sarah squealed, "was Maria our *mother*? I thought you two didn't meet until college. What happened after you first saw her in Primary?"

I looked across the room to see Maria's response to the question, but she was no longer there. At first I thought she had gone to prepare refreshments, but when she didn't come back, I supposed she had gone on up to bed. It wasn't until sometime later that I learned the *real* reason for her leaving the room. In the meantime, I was left to my own devices to explain why we hadn't told the children about this early encounter between us.

"Well," I replied, not wanting to mislead them, "we were pretty young when we met, not much past five or so. So, if I hadn't heard my parents repeat the story as an amusing incident from my childhood, I doubt I would have even remembered it. Only my mother's wanting to save the picture as a reminder of the event left me with a memento of it. Besides," I added honestly, "without our names on the back of this photo, we probably still wouldn't have made the connection years later when we were dating."

All of this was true, but it masked the *real* story, and that bothered me. Still, the full truth about our first meeting was something their mother had chosen not to discuss with them--at least at this point in her life. Somehow, as I sat there, I felt the time was coming when she would be ready to give them more information than she had in the past. But for now, I simply dodged the question by saying that their mother had moved out of town within a year or so after the picture was taken. "To our knowledge," I concluded, "we didn't see each other again until we were in college."

The kids seemed satisfied with the explanation, at least for the time being. After visiting for a few more minutes, I suggested that it was time for bed. And so, offering a brief closing prayer--and pulling a package of red licorice out of my desk drawer for a treat--I suggested the kids go and give their mother a big hug, then be off to bed. Strangely, they offered no resistance, and I soon found myself alone in my study.

After tidying up, I went to our bedroom to find Maria. To my surprise, she was in the bathroom cleaning the sink. It was nine o'clock at night, and she was cleaning the *sink*! At that moment I knew something was terribly wrong! Before I could even get a word out, however, she snapped, "Richard, I couldn't believe you told that story about our Primary meeting without even consulting me! You know how I feel about my childhood. It seems to me that when *I'm* ready, *I* should be the one to explain it to the kids!"

Somewhat defensively, I pleaded my case. "Maria, it seemed so harmless. . . ."

That was when the realization hit me about Maria's recent behavior. Her *past* was still haunting her, and now she was taking it out on us. It also worried me that her anger toward her father was spilling into the most important parts of her life, and I had no way to stem the tide.

Still, making a stab into the dark, I asked, "Maria, don't you think it's about time you helped the kids understand your early life? After all, you don't have anything to be embarrassed about. You didn't make your father's decision to walk away from you and your mother. And besides, you haven't really spoken to him since you were eight. I don't think there is much to say about a divorce that occurred several decades ago."

"Richard, it isn't fair that you tell me how *I* should feel!" Her response was predictably short. Then, without letting me explain myself, she added, "I think that I should have the right to decide *if* and *when* I fill in the details about my life to the children without pressure from *you*."

Not wanting to prolong the discussion about this apparently still unresolvable conflict, I shrugged my shoulders in agreement. I knew the time would come when these troubling issues for Maria, as well as her growing anger, would have to be addressed. But I also knew that it would have to be on *her* timetable, not mine.

While Maria and I didn't spend much time during the next several weeks talking about her feelings, the contents of the box continued to spark a spirit of intrigue among the kids. Within a week of the Family Home Evening lesson from the treasure box, our third son, Luke, decided to take the box to school for show-and-tell. He later told me that he thought his classmates would be very impressed with his story telling ability--*if* he could tell stories in the magical way he had experienced. His plan might have gotten to the show-and-tell stage, too, if I hadn't gone to my study just after he left for school and noticed that the box was missing. When I asked Sarah about it in the kitchen, she said that he had just walked out the door juggling it in a garbage sack.

I barely intercepted Luke at the school door and kindly convinced him that an attempt at supernatural storytelling skills could go awry, leaving him embarrassed rather than looking like a hero. I also tried to let him know that I just might be the only one who could tell the stories in such vivid detail. After all, I added, the experiences *did* happen to me, and all the details were probably locked somewhere in my mind. Reluctantly he bought my explanation, then apologized for taking the box without my permission.

Over the next several weeks, mostly without Maria in attendance, I continued to have unusual experiences with the kids and the box. I would unlock it and open the lid. Then retrieving one of my treasures, I would share my memory of receiving it, together with an applicable lesson.

For example, one afternoon the kids were playing on the trampoline, and there was an accident that required Walter to have several stitches. After he and Maria returned from the emergency room, Maria tried to explain to all the children that *each* of them shared responsibility for the accident. Her efforts were without effect, however, as each defended his side of the story.

As Maria later recounted it, the justifying went on and on, until finally, in exasperation, she told both boys that when I returned from work, I would deal with it.

"Oh good," Luke exclaimed with complete frustration. "Maybe Dad'll have a story from the box to help us!"

"Yeah," Walter countered, "and then you'll see why it was all your *fault!*"

"Well," Maria snapped just as I was walking into the house, "maybe some day you'll each take responsibility, instead of always passing the blame!"

No sooner did I walk through the door than I was bombarded with two versions of the same story with no one at fault. After dinner, we all went upstairs to talk about what had happened. I knew the kids expected me to solve this with an incident from the box, and I hoped I could come up with just the right story. Glancing at the items in the bottom of the chest, my eyes were drawn to a package of unused firecrackers. *I wonder if these will help*, I considered hesitantly. As I lifted the package into the air, an immediate stir came from the kids, especially from the boys. And then I began to recount an event that until this moment lay buried in the far recesses of my mind. . . .

11

*I*t's Not My Fault,

It's In My Jeans

"Ricky, are you all right? Ricky . . . Ricky!"

Shaking my head, I looked up at Kent as I tried to get my bearings. "What happened, Kent?" I asked, then added, "Boy, does my head hurt!"

"Don't you remember?" he replied, a little concerned at my loss of memory.

"No, tell me again . . . please!"

This time as he began to describe our adventure, I recalled what had happened. Then I realized that Lee was standing next to Kent, and it all came back to me. Only moments before, we were huddled in the middle of the street where we were putting almost all the firecrackers into a number ten can. We had carefully taken the obvious precautions to avoid detection: we were on a side street; we had found a large can in which to put the firecrackers; and we had made sure that there were no little children in sight.

The three of us placed the can in the middle of the street. We then tied several of the strings of firecrackers together. Placing the packet of small explosives inside the can, we carefully lit the fuses, then ran to the curb. Seconds later, we enjoyed one of the loudest, most exhilarating explosions ever! And the can? Well, that was the best part! When it landed back on the road, it resembled a hamburger bun--flat on the top and bottom, and all puffed out in the middle.

That was when we saw a dark figure right across the street standing next to a car. "Let's get outta here!" someone yelled. Needless to say, we bolted in three different directions. Unfortunately, I was looking over my shoulder at the mysterious intruder as I ran helter-skelter in the opposite direction. I didn't think about the large maple tree until I had picked up too much speed to avoid running smack-dab into it and dropping like a dead weight. That's when Kent and Lee came running back to see what had happened. Fortunately, my memory gradually returned.

At the same time the apparent stranger walked slowly across the street to speak with us. To our considerable surprise, the *stranger* was Sister Anna Pritchard, our Primary teacher. Finding that there was no permanent damage to my head, she called each of us by name and gathered us around her. "Young men," she said in a patronizing way, "what do you have to say for yourselves?"

In response, we tried the Garden of Eden defense. You know it and have probably used it yourself. *No one's guilty but the serpent!* First, Kent and Lee pointed out that they were just along for the ride. The firecrackers weren't theirs-- neither were the can nor the matches. Besides, they added, it was all set up in front of my house, far from theirs. In short, their fingers of guilt were pointed directly at me. I also had a ready-made excuse, unfortunately I didn't blame the serpent.

"Sister Pritchard," I barked, "it's not *my* fault! Why, it's in my jeans!"

"In your genes, Richard?" she asked incredulously. "What could you possibly mean? You're not really trying to claim that you inherited a tendency for illegal pyrotechnics, are you?"

49

At first, I didn't understand what she meant, but then I remembered a discussion in science class about genes, so I quickly responded, "Oh, no, Sister Pritchard, not those genes . . . *these*."

I pointed down at my pants, wishing her idea of an inheritance excuse had occurred to me first. But, sensing that I was on a roll, I quickly added, "Yesterday I found these old pants up in the attic, and the pockets were filled with firecrackers. All kinds of stuff, you know . . . M-80s, cherry bombs, snakes . . . the works!"

Sister Pritchard didn't for one minute buy into my jeans story. She just gathered up the rest of our illegal fireworks and walked across the street with them in her hands. As she was getting into her car, she seemed to be smiling, when she added, "Young men, I'll see you next Wednesday at Primary. Our lesson will be on spiritual *jean*-etics."

As promised, when we arrived at Primary the following week, Sister Pritchard invited us to read some scriptures about free agency, choice-making, and being accountable for our actions. We had worried about her lesson all week, and my stomach was tied in knots until class was over.

Finally, as the class period was drawing to a close, she concluded by saying, "Our Heavenly Father gave us the right and the power to make choices. This power is one of the Lord's most valuable gifts, and he will not take it away from us."

Well, that was all the set-up. Continuing, she added the kicker that nearly cut us to the quick. "Now, boys," she said in a louder-than-normal voice, "you also need to remember this: Heavenly Father will always hold us accountable for the consequences *of* those choices. . . ."

After a brief pause, she asked if anyone had gotten the meaning of what she had said. "Bruce," (she called on Bruce when she wanted the best answers), "what do *you* think that means?"

As usual, Bruce had been paying careful attention. In fact, he had the right answer so often that some of us wondered if he had his own copy of the lesson manual. His response was something like, "Oh, I think the Lord wants to see if we'll do what we're supposed to while were down here on earth. The challenge is that we can't see Him all the time like we used to. If we do make the right choices, then we will make it back to live with Him. If we don't, then we won't. It's that simple!"

Sister Pritchard nodded approvingly, added a few brief comments, then concluded her lesson.

I never knew where Bruce came up with his answers. He did it often enough, however, that he saved the rest of us from embarrassing ourselves.

Later that night, I kept trying to understand what Sister Pritchard was saying. I came to the conclusion that there were two lessons involved: first, if we don't do what the Lord tells us to do, we're gonna *get it*; and second, if we make a bad choice, we must accept responsibility *for* the choice--and not blame it on our jeans!

With that, I sneaked up stairs to the attic and found something I had stashed away--just in case. After turning on the light and searching for a few minutes, I found my cache--one package of unused firecrackers. But they were no longer in my jeans, and I knew that whatever happened next would be my responsibility. Wisely, I decided to hide them in my treasure box.

Slipping quietly into my room, I pulled the box out from under the bed. After opening it and finding just the right compartment, I sat there imagining another date with destiny and firecrackers.

12

*T*o *Be Or*
Not To Be

Gripping the old and faded firecrackers in my hands, I blinked a few times, and there in front of me were my five children looking at the old package of M-80's with wide-eyed excitement. Now I don't know if hearing this story helped them understand accountability, but we *did* have fun talking about it. They also marveled, as did Maria and I, at the vividness of the mental images we could all see as the story unfolded. I will also admit that I was tempted by their entreaties to sneak out behind the house with a number ten can and try to repeat the pyrotechnic magic of that evening. But after talking about it further, we concluded that we shouldn't go about destroying any of the contents of the treasure box until after we figured out its mystery.

Not long after this, I was looking through the box and found the skeleton of a sand crab in a bottle. Later that night, again with Maria conspicuously absent, I used the sand crab to help the older children solve a problem. It seems that one of the nonmember families in Mendon was about to join the Church. Unfortunately, the children in this family had a very bad reputation at their elementary school. They were socially backward and were often very unkind.

After a dinnertime conversation where Walter, Sarah, *and* Luke speculated that the Lord had made a mistake in sending the missionaries to the McTeel's house, I decided that we should retire to my study and open up the box. Fortunately, the unique feeling that came while listening to the stories had not been dimmed by overuse, so the kids agreed to listen. What they *didn't* agree to was changing their feelings about the McTeels. As soon as we entered the study, Walter picked up the box and handed it to me. By this time we had a mutual agreement that I was the only one who could open the Chest--simply because I didn't want to prematurely reveal the rest of the treasures. Anyway, this time when I opened the box, I didn't have to search for anything. Forcing my thoughts away from a now almost never-present Maria, I simply reached down and picked up the bottle containing the sand crab skeleton. As I did, I began to describe an incident that, when it transpired, was fraught with anxiety.

In a manner that was by now becoming as familiar as it was strange, a scene long-forgotten came into view. As the setting became visible to each of us, I was filled with youthful emotions of inferiority mixed with fear. Gradually, I began to describe what I was seeing and feeling. . . .

13

*B*uddy Ramsey

Meets Godzilla

"Ricky," Mom spoke my name gently, then added, "you are *very* special. . . ."

"Well, I don't *feel* special," I honestly replied. "I'm always chosen last in games at school; I can't read as well as my friends, and I don't think I'll ever understand two-place division."

"Now, Richard," she responded kindly, while using my formal name to make me feel more grown-up, "you're only in fourth grade, and everything hasn't been decided yet." Then continuing, she suddenly changed the subject. "But, you've really got to hurry, or you'll be late for Primary."

That's right, I remembered, *it is Primary day, so I'd better get a move on.*

Jumping up, I grabbed my coat, gave Mom a hug, then headed out my bedroom door and down the hallway. Once outside, I looked around for Conrad, my always faithful dog, who liked to follow me to Primary. But he was nowhere to be found. I was running late, so I couldn't spend time looking for him. Besides, the chapel was just four blocks from our house, so it wasn't a big deal for a ten-year-old to walk up the street alone.

Today, however, it was a bigger deal than I could have ever imagined. About halfway to the chapel, on the same side of the street, lived my old nemesis, Buddy Ramsey. Buddy was the meanest guy in our school. And he was huge, too--as in *King Kong* huge! Some kids said he had gotten his growth early. I wasn't sure exactly what that meant, but I did agree--it *had* come a little soon for me.

For protection, I followed the notion that the best defense was to blend into the landscape and just stay out of Buddy's way. And throughout my early years at George Washington Elementary, I usually managed to keep out of his direct line of fire. But, as you probably recall, Buddy had given me fits a time or two before. You may remember that day at the Swedish Temple several years ago. And more recently, there was the afternoon when I received my forest green Trail Blazer bandalo.

Over the years, Buddy knocked books out of my hands several times at the bus stop. But before you think I was someone *special*, let me add that Buddy did that to almost everyone at the bus stop. Even so, I didn't think Buddy really even knew who I was. It's the role of a bully to torment his victims, not identify them.

Well anyway, there I was, walking up the street toward Primary, getting unwittingly closer to a personal crisis. As I crossed the last intersection before reaching Buddy's house, I looked up. And wouldn't you know it--there he was! He was playing with his gigantic dog, Nosty. That's right, Nosty--it's spelled with an "o," not an "a," although either spelling would fit *this* beast.

Nosty was Buddy's enormous Labrador Retriever. Buddy didn't come up with the name, however. The story was that his older brother named the dog upon returning from college one summer. It seems that the name "Nosty" was short for Nostrodomos, who was some kind of a prophet--not a church prophet, as you probably know, but some other kind.

Buddy's brother said that the dog wasn't exactly a prophet, but he *could* change someone's future. That took no further explanation, even for a fifth grader.

Because Nosty was about the biggest and meanest dog my friends and I had ever seen, we all stayed out of his way. Isn't that the way it always goes? The biggest, meanest bully owns the biggest, meanest dog! It wouldn't make sense for a nerd to own a wolf, or for a bully to own a gentle cocker spaniel. Even so, it *would* help even out the odds. I owned a dog named Conrad, but he was like a lamb compared to Nosty. And Conrad was somewhere back home, so he provided no comfort whatsoever during this moment of peril.

As I kept walking down the street toward these twin forces of evil, I tried to blend in with nature. *Maybe I can just look like a small moving tree, or a blade of grass, and he won't notice me.* But my thoughts were to no avail. Buddy didn't just *notice* me--he began *staring* at me! Then his face lit up with a grin so big I began to tremble. Suddenly he whistled for Nosty. When the dog joined him, Buddy grabbed him by the collar and started walking directly toward me.

I couldn't believe that I had gotten myself into this fix. Normally after school, Buddy was working down at the family cleaners. It was known that all of his family, including his grandfather, were members of the Church, although they never attended. They owned a laundry about a mile from their house, and they all seemed to work there. That meant Buddy was almost never home after school.

Everyone knew Buddy's work schedule, but it still wasn't worth the risk to walk past his house. Why, even if Buddy weren't home, Nosty could quite possibly be lurking in the bushes. So, what was I doing walking on Buddy's side of the street, when a wise fifth-grader would have crossed to the other side several houses back? Frankly, I just forgot, and now here I was, in the biggest fix of my life!

You see, Tommy Richards had brought a sand crab in a

bottle to school that day for show-and-tell. He told us that he had named him Godzilla, which really added to everyone's interest. On the bus ride home, after a little coaxing, Tommy said I could take it to my house--if I would bring it with me to Primary. And so, while walking to Primary, I had become so interested in the sand crab in the bottle that I hadn't remembered to take a safer route--or at least walk on the other side of the street. Now, as Buddy and Nosty grew closer and closer, I looked into the bottle and wondered if this beach creature were an *attack* sand crab. *Doubtful,* I reasoned quickly. *I'm a goner, for sure!*

At that moment I found myself in double jeopardy. The sand crab was about to become the property of the meanest boy in our elementary school, and I was about to be eaten by the meanest dog in the neighborhood! While my very life was flashing before my eyes, I took some consolation in knowing I wouldn't have to explain to Tommy what had happened to his sand crab. After all, no such explanations are required after one's untimely departure into the Spirit World!

I was only one house away from Buddy's yard when the silent prayers I had been offering were miraculously answered. From out of nowhere, my older brother, Ted, appeared. I later learned that he had been following along behind me, just out of sight. In my mental state I hadn't noticed him. Ted was in the seventh grade. He had gotten his growth earlier than Buddy, and had gotten even more of it. Ted had just graduated from Primary, and as it turned out, was on his way to help the Guide Patrol with a scouting activity.

Sensing my dilemma, he immediately called out my name. "Ricky, what's in the bottle?" Without waiting for my reply, he quickly caught up with me and held out his hand. Gratefully and silently I handed him the bottle containing the sand crab which he examined briefly and handed back to me.

"Do you want to walk with me to Primary, Ricky?" Ted

asked, while putting his arm on my shoulder. That was the first time I realized that Ted had probably seen the blossoming crisis as he walked along behind me and had waited until just the right moment to make his appearance.

"Of course," I echoed, trying to act nonchalant without knowing exactly what that meant.

As we got right in front of Buddy's house, we could see him walking toward the side yard, away from us. No doubt he'd seen Ted join me and thought better of his evil plan. Surprisingly, and with genuine enthusiasm, Ted called out to him, "Hey, Buddy, why don't you put Nosty away and come to Primary with us?!"

With that invitation, Buddy turned around and surprised both of us. "Just a minute," he yelled. And in about that time he was back, walking along the street with us. Then with remarkable candor, he said, "You know, I've always wanted to go to Primary, but my folks always make me work at the laundry. Today, though, the big machines are being fixed, so I snuck out. No one will even miss me."

Without waiting for a response, he added, "I thought about going to Primary today, but I just couldn't. I felt a little weird about going alone, because it's been so long since I've been inside the church. I thought the other kids would say things; then I'd get mad, and. . . ."

In mid-sentence, Buddy looked down and saw my bottle. "What's in the bottle, Squirt?" Somehow the name "Squirt" didn't make me feel small, as it had in the past when he called me that. This time it seemed to be a special nickname from one friend to another. So I handed him the bottle and told him that it was a sand crab that had come all the way from a beach near Galveston, Texas. He looked at it briefly, then handed it back, telling me that it was a pretty neat pet.

We soon arrived at the chapel, and before I knew it, we were are sitting in our classes. Afterward the three of us walked together as far as Buddy's house. Along the way Buddy talked about maybe going to Primary the following week if he could figure out a way to convince his parents to let him off work. He told us that he really liked scouting. Taking a cue from Buddy's concerns, Ted volunteered to get our mom to talk to Buddy's mother, then maybe she *would* let him go.

After we separated and Ted and I were walking home, I couldn't help thinking about this brother of mine and the events of the day. Somehow he appeared out of nowhere with just the right approach to change Buddy's intentions-- and save *my* bacon as well as *Tommy's* sand crab.

14

T o Become Acceptable

Our son, Luke, was the first to recognize Buddy
Ramsey's name. He recalled that Buddy was the bully that
had caused me pain and difficulty on a number of other
occasions. Long before the story was completed, all the
children acknowledged that Buddy Ramsey was a real
scoundrel who should have been fed to his dog, Nosty.
While we laughed about the idea, I was certain that the
older children had gotten the message.

That assurance was confirmed when Sarah innocently
asked, "Daddy, where is Buddy Ramsey today?"

"Well," I replied, reaching back into my memory, "he
started attending Primary fairly regularly from that week on.
He continued on into the Young Men's program. Earning
his Eagle Scout rank helped him, no doubt, as did the caring
concern of some great youth leaders. After his mission and
college, he settled right back in town, and today he spends
his mornings and afternoons terrorizing young children at
the bus stops all around town."

Only Elizabeth bought into what I said. Walter

challenged it immediately. "Come on, Dad," he protested, "you wouldn't have told a story without a good ending! What *really* happened to him?"

"Well, would you believe that he took over the family business, continued to be active in Church, and now serves as bishop of the very ward Ted brought him back to?"

Sarah then spoke. "So, I suppose you think we should look at the McTeels as potential Buddy Ramseys, right?" She was correct in reminding us that the *real* story here was about a seemingly unacceptable, even embarrassing family right here in Mendon who were seeking the light of the gospel.

"I hadn't thought of it exactly like that, Sarah, but you've got the general idea. I just wanted all of you to think about how *you* would need to be treated, if you were Buddy Ramsey."

With that explanation to consider, and with Maria having gone to bed earlier with what I feared was a contrived headache, I gathered the kids for prayer. Afterward, we all went to bed a little bit more resolved to help the McTeels. The thrilling thing for us was that two weeks later the entire McTeel family was baptized into the Church. Not only that, but we were all there to give our support. Now, I don't want to say that they turned into finished products right away. In fact, today some of the children still act more like Nosty in his prime than a grown-up Buddy Ramsey. But they've become permanent members, and we're growing to love them.

Their baptism was a very sweet service and reminded us all of how the gospel can work in our lives. In fact, a few days afterward I was sitting in my den thinking about the blessings of repentance and turning over a new leaf. One thought led to another and I began considering all that Maria had accomplished since we'd been married. I remembered her excellent service as relief society president in New York City. Notwithstanding what I now was discovering about her troubled heart, she had accepted the calling without hesitation, and served faithfully. She did this even though she kept the pain from her youth bottled up inside. On the outside, however, people viewed Maria and me--as well as our family--as one of those Teflon, trouble-free families. However, both Maria and I were very private people, and I suppose our children have taken after us. We haven't given press releases about our successes, and neither have we worn our challenges on our sleeves. Thus, while Maria has served in the Church wherever we have lived, she hasn't served without personal strain and difficulty--even though she has kept it to herself.

Although I couldn't see it right at the time, these episodes from the box were gradually breaking through the veneer that had covered Maria for a long, long time. One particular example comes to mind. . . .

Recently, after what had been a very difficult day for me, Maria and I slipped into the study and were unwinding--just visiting about odds and ends. Suddenly our daughter Sarah entered the room with a rather troubled look on her face. Apparently she had just been speaking on the phone with a good friend who was a member of our ward. They had been talking about repentance and the atonement.

"Dad," she interrupted, "how can Heavenly Father ever overlook our past deeds? After all, they're a part of us. I think we can ask Him to forgive us, but the effects seem there to stay."

"Sarah," I inappropriately barked, "didn't you see that your mother and I were talking?"

"Uh . . . sorry, Dad, it's just that. . . ."

Realizing that I had jumped on Sarah unjustly, I interrupted her and apologized. I then said, "Please tell me what's driving your thoughts, Honey."

"Okay. Well, you know Anna. . . . Her father has been inactive for a *long* time, and she's hoping beyond hope that he will come back someday. We've been talking about repentance in Seminary, but we haven't heard anything that convinces either of us that her father can actually get all the way *back* into the Church."

"So, you want to know how repentance works, right?"

"Right!" Sarah's countenance instantly lit up, and I was relieved that I hadn't offended her. Looking past me, she suddenly focused on the treasure box and exclaimed, "Gee, Dad, I'll bet there's something in there that'll help me understand!"

Then, without even looking for confirmation from me, she expectantly picked up the box and handed it to me. Sensing that she was right, I opened it at once and peered down inside. My eyes immediately made contact with a piece of wood that was wrapped in a wrinkled sheet of white paper. Pulling it out, I juggled it briefly in my hands. Then, while a very quiet Maria listened, I spoke to Sarah of a time long past.

Holding the piece of wood and the white sheet of paper in my hands, and with a clarity that was becoming increasingly familiar, I related an incident that until now had been forgotten. This experience had forever changed my understanding of the atonement. In some strange way, I began to examine these questions again, as if the answers were coming to me--and to Maria--for the very first time.

15

Of Boards, Nails

and Wrinkles

Holding my brown bag for an entire class period did nothing to remove the concerns I was carrying along with the contents of the sack. I knew I was completely preoccupied with my questions, because I hardly heard a word Sister Hamlin said during her lesson. But I think she knew something important was on my mind, because she didn't even once comment about my lack of participation. Then before I knew it, she was calling on someone to offer the closing prayer. Thankfully, that *someone* wasn't me!

Allowing my other classmates to exit the room without me, I very cautiously picked up my brown bag and headed to the front where she was putting her things away.

"Sister Hamlin," I spoke slowly, almost in a whisper, "could you please help me?"

"Well, of course, dear," she smiled. "What do you need?"

"Actually, I need you to explain something to all of us in the class. We've argued about this on the bus and stuff. When I went to my dad, he said he could do it. But he also said that you were a much better teacher than he is, so perhaps you could do it better."

"My goodness," she exclaimed as her heavily mascara'd lashes lifted slightly. "Isn't your father one for flattery?! Well, what do you have in your sack?"

Setting the large, burlap bag down on the floor, I slowly pulled it open. I then extracted three items--a hammer, a large nail, and a board. Placing the board down on the floor, I picked up the hammer and immediately began pounding the nail down into it. Sister Hamlin didn't say anything, but stood quietly, wondering what I would do next.

After burying the nail about a half inch into the board, I stopped hammering, pulled the nail out, then commenced to pound it in not more than an inch from the previous hole. Repeating this process three more times, I finally stopped, placed my hammer back inside the bag, and looked up. Sister Hamlin was sitting quietly on the chair above me with her eyes intently fixed on me and the board.

"Sister Hamlin, I once had another teacher who taught me that sinning is like putting another hole in the board of my life. She said that once the hole is there, even if I repent, I will always carry the scar of that sin. In other words, because of the hole, I can never be completely *whole* again."

"My goodness, Richard," she coughed. "You've really been thinking about this, haven't you?"

"Yes, and when I asked Dad about it, he was patient and all, but said that if I asked you, you would probably teach a good lesson about it to everyone in class. Sometimes I think there are too many 'lessons' when I just want to know the answer: is my life like this board, or not?"

"Besides," I continued, gaining more confidence the longer I spoke, "I don't think it's fair. Do you? I mean, if I truly repent, then why do I have to keep the black mark up in heaven?"

"Actually, my young friend," she replied in her special way that made me feel accepted, "I was planning to give a lesson on repentance soon, so I'll just switch things around and give it next Wednesday. Can you wait that long for an answer?"

"Sure, that'll be great," I sighed, relieved that she hadn't asked me any more about sinning . . . especially about *my* sins!

With that, I placed the board back into the bag, bid her farewell, and was out of the room before she could say "Jack Robinson." I had done what Dad had asked me to do, and I had survived. Now I would just wait to see what the next week's lesson would bring.

The week passed quickly, and before I knew it, I was back in that classroom, waiting for the lesson to begin. When Sister Hamlin saw me enter into the room, she winked, but said nothing to me. Finally, after calling on Ronnie Jacobson to offer the opening prayer, she stood and faced the class.

"Boys," she began, again flashing her ever-present smile, "today we're going to talk about repentance and forgiveness. I've been thinking a lot about this principle lately, and I hope you like what I have to share with you."

Holding up a sheet of white paper, she continued speaking. "Boys, today we're going to talk about making mistakes, or sinning, and what happens next. If your life were represented on this sheet of paper at age eight, or the time that you were baptized, you would see yourself free from wrinkles, or scars of sin. Since then, however-- especially if you are like me--I suspect you've made mistakes on a fairly regular basis. Each of these mistakes, or sins, can be represented by an additional wrinkle in the paper."

Stopping briefly, Sister Hamlin begin to wrinkle the sheet of paper in her hands. "Now," she continued, "some of you might think that when you repent, the wrinkles remain--even when you try to smooth out the sheet of paper."

Without trying to embarrass me, Sister Hamlin then proceeded to talk about our private discussion and about my board and nail demonstration the week before. She taught us that through repentance it is as though we were given a new board, or a new life, without any holes. After she finished talking about the nail holes, she picked up a second piece of white paper. Holding it carefully by the corners, she said, "Now, boys, I want you always to remember this clean sheet of paper. In reality, no matter what sins you commit, so long as you don't take the life of another person, your sin can be completely removed from the record Heavenly Father is keeping up in heaven. You don't have to carry the scars, for He has promised that He will remember them no more."

When she asked for questions, I couldn't believe how fast the hands flew into the air. My friends had more questions than I ever anticipated, and I slowly began to relax. I had really felt the pressure while she was talking about my nail demonstration, and I was glad she was back with the paper.

"Now," she finally concluded, "I have a gift for each of you." She then gave each of us a piece of paper and had us repeat the demonstration of squashing it into a ball, then smoothing it all out. She next surprised us by handing each of us a manila envelope with the flap still open.

"Boys," she said gently, "inside each of your envelopes is a another piece of paper with absolutely no wrinkles at all. Place the wrinkled one inside your envelope, then take them both home and teach this lesson to your family. I'm sure they'll all appreciate how *complete* repenting and forgiving are."

With that, she shared her testimony of how Jesus forgives us our sins when we promise not to repeat them. She then called on me to give the closing prayer. Well, I'm not much on praying, as I often told my dad, but on that Wednesday I gave one of the my best prayers ever. It wasn't just one of those "thank you and bless us" prayers, but was truly a prayer from my heart. I asked Heavenly Father to help each of us repent of any mistakes we had made--including the way we had thrown some rotten duck eggs on Sister Hamlin's front porch. Concluding, I asked him to help us have faith in the lesson we had just learned, so that we would have a clear conscience.

The following Sunday afternoon my dad let me share this story with the whole family. At the conclusion of my lesson, I took the manila envelope and opened it so that I could read aloud the words that Sister Hamlin had carefully crafted on the clean and unwrinkled sheet of paper. The words, spoken by Isaiah, were, *Though your sins be as scarlet, they shall become white as snow.*

After the lesson, I sneaked up to my bedroom and carefully pulled my treasure chest out from under my bed. Carefully wrapping a piece of wood with nail holes with a wrinkled sheet of paper, I placed them in one of the compartments that Uncle ValGene carefully crafted years before. Then, in the adjacent compartment, I place a coiled manila envelope containing the pure white paper with the words of Isaiah written on it. In doing so, I wondered if I would ever really use this box when I grew older. A strange thought for a ten-year-old, I know, but why else what was I saving all this stuff, anyway?

16

*A*nother Difficult Call

When I finished relating this story, Sarah remarked that the illustration was very helpful. "In fact," she maturely added, "I can make my own board and paper illustration to show Megan as I explain that her father can truly repent of his past and be forgiven. I think that will be a great comfort to her, and maybe she'll use these illustrations to teach her father the way back. You never know." She then thanked me for helping her better understand the truth about repentance and walked from the room. I sat there in my chair for a few moments thinking about how well my life had been going--except, of course, for the growing helplessness I felt about Maria.

I had been serving as ward Young Men's president for several months now, and I had enjoyed it immensely. In truth, it hadn't been as difficult as I thought it would be to balance my time between family, church, and work. Although it was challenging to be so helpless in supporting Maria, somehow Heavenly Father influenced my days and enabled me to get more done in less time, or so it seemed to me. I wondered then, and I still wonder, if time isn't somehow stretched or multiplied so that the important things get done.

Well, that's how I was feeling until the phone rang. It was the stake executive secretary asking for me. We began a somewhat casual conversation as he reminded me that Stake Conference was the following weekend. I appreciated the reminder, but was certain that wasn't the purpose of his call. He then proceeded to ask if I could meet with the stake presidency on Saturday night following the evening conference session. Immediately my stomach turned into a Gordian knot--one that I knew could not easily be cut. Not only was I not going to relax after the call, but the puzzle was: why did they want to see *me*?

After we concluded our conversation, I told Maria whom I had been speaking with and of the invitation that had been extended. I further indicated that she had been asked to be present. Repressing her own fears, she asked, "Well, dear, are you in some kind of trouble?"

"Probably. . . ." I somehow sensed that my life was about to change dramatically. At first I considered the alternatives and hoped that I was going to be asked to serve as a stake clerk. I loved those out-of-the-limelight and under-control positions. But in my heart-of-hearts, I knew that such was not to be the case. In a quiet moment later that night, the Spirit whispered information that I really didn't want to hear. *Richard, you are to be called to preside as bishop of the Mendon Ward.*

I knew down deep that this was true, and although I feared for Maria's reaction to the call more than for myself, somehow I felt a calming influence of the Spirit as I privately petitioned the Lord regarding it.

The two days passed quickly, and before I knew it, Maria and I were sitting in the stake president's office. After asking briefly about my personal worthiness--and after asking for, then receiving, Maria's support--President Hayes did indeed extend a call to me to serve as bishop. Even so,

70

in no way did my premonitions prepare me for the shock waves that suddenly passed through me. An hour later, as we drove home from the stake center, there was total quiet in the car. In spite of Maria's feelings about *herself,* I could sense her support and appreciation that I was found worthy to be called to such a position. When we arrived home, I told Maria that I wanted to spend a little time in my office, by myself. It seemed appropriate to both of us, so she graciously kissed me goodnight at the top of the stairs, and I walked into my study. I had desperately wanted to talk with her about her emotions, and about the increasing *distancing* I had noticed in her behavior with not only me, but with everyone. But still I felt constrained, so I focused on the crucial task of selecting my counselors.

To say that I was overwhelmed by this new calling would be a gross understatement. As I thought about the changes this would bring in my life--as well as in the lives of Maria and the kids--I recalled my feelings when I was asked to serve as Young Men's president. The dilemma of time management had been faced and solved, but with this new calling came feelings of inability and loneliness. *How can I ever do this*? I asked myself. *I'm just not prepared. If I had known sooner that this was coming, I would have lived a different life--and I would have pressed harder to have Maria come to grips with her past. I know some bishops who seem to have been working their entire life to be ready to serve, but this has come as a total surprise to me. I just don't think I'm ready.*

I learned later that these feelings of inadequacy were common among bishops, especially before they were sustained, ordained, and the power of the mantle was placed upon their shoulders. Sitting there on the sofa, I could only think about my apparent inability to do what was going to be required of me. While doing so, I found myself looking fondly at my old treasure box. In an instant I felt a surge of reassurance, and in one movement I reached for the box and opened the lid.

Peering down into the partitions, I quickly noticed a small, plastic row boat with two oars. My parents had given it to me many years before as a memento of a milestone event that happened shortly after my eighth birthday. As I picked up the small boat, I could suddenly see a familiar dining room table where I was sitting, staring off into space.

17

*F*aith Works

There I was sitting at the breakfast table, lost in a daydream of an eight-year-old about becoming a star athlete instead of focusing on the one of the biggest problems of my life. *Boy,* I wondered to myself, *what's happening to me? My daydreams are so real! Could I really ever become a high school basketball star? Actually doubtful, I'd say.*

Pulling myself quickly out of my fantasy and back into the present, I gulped down the last spoonful of Cream of Wheat cereal. I felt a knot forming in my stomach that had little to do with my breakfast. It was Sunday morning, and the sky outside was sunny and clear. Yet I was filled with a sense of foreboding. I just *knew* that this morning would be one of the most difficult of my entire life. Little did I realize that in the next few hours I would learn more about faith and works than I had ever bargained for.

I was about to give my first talk in Senior Sunday School. With all of my training in Primary, you'd have thought that I'd be able to breeze confidently through my first public speaking assignment in mortality. To the contrary--I was becoming sicker by the minute, and deep inside my crowded mind, my memorized lines were beginning to fade mysteriously into oblivion. And why had I been forced to memorize my talk? You can be sure it wasn't *my* idea. It was my dad's brainstorm. He had insisted and imposed such a burden simply because, as he told me, he was on the stake high council. He insisted that more was expected of his children because of it. His explanation seemed reasonable enough, except for the fact that *I* wasn't on the high council, and everyone knew that!

One afternoon, when I returned home from mowing Widow Kendell's lawn, Dad informed me that the Sunday School president had called and asked that I speak in Senior Sunday School the following week. He told me that my mother had accepted the assignment for me, knowing that I would have accepted had I been home to do so!

Well, I was stunned speechless when Dad informed me of this unexpected "blessing." *Pretty ugly disguise for a blessing*, I moaned silently. Dad went on to explain that, as a newly baptized member of the Savior's Church, I had a greater obligation to do such things! I hadn't as yet grasped the full meaning of the concept of free agency, but somehow in my young mind I knew that if this were an example of it, then free agency wasn't really free. Still, the task was at hand, and Dad assured me that he would help me write my talk.

Even though he did help me--why, he even wrote my words on 3"X 5" cards--the talk was still *mine* to memorize and then deliver! In spite of all my preparation, I felt just awful. You see, other than memorizing such useful things as where my mom hid the candy and cookies in the house, I had never memorized *anything* in my life. But here I was, gearing up for a grand performance that would likely kill me from fright--that is, if I didn't die of worry before Sunday arrived!

Sunday did arrive, however, and although I was still alive, it was just barely. I think my stomach felt worse than it did the day we sneaked into Widow Kendall's apple orchard and ate about a bushel of green apples. When I announced my sickness to my mom and told her that I wouldn't be able to give the talk that day, she just smiled and nodded her head. She then told me to exercise faith, do the best I could, and leave my health up to the Lord. Pretty tough for a newly baptized member to resist all that logic! I was trapped! I knew it; I knew she knew it; and now the only way out was to give the talk and be done with it!

A half hour later, my numb, nauseated, and seemingly tortured body walked the few blocks to the meetinghouse. Anyone looking at me would have thought I was filled with confidence. Why, I was sporting my new gray-rimmed glasses, my shoes were finely polished, and I was wearing my big brother's hand-me-down white shirt and a brand-new gray and maroon bow tie! In short, I was decked out in grand religious style--except, of course, for the squadron of Monarch butterflies that had taken flight somewhere inside my mush-filled stomach!

Soon my high council father and I were seated on the stand at the front of our chapel. He was to hold the 3"X 5" cards and prompt me if I couldn't remember what to say next during my talk. I don't know why he didn't trust *me* to hold them. After all I was a big boy, and could prompt myself just fine. "Great speakers don't look at their notes," he told me. It seemed a stretch to call a rookie like me a *great* anything.

"Anyway," he added, "the cards will only serve as a crutch." Whatever *that* meant!

Minutes passed, and before I knew it, my name was being announced as the only person to be giving a talk. Evidently the other person assigned--a girl, no less--had gotten sick and so was unable to be there. *Likely story*, I thought to myself. *The only difference between her and me is that her mother let her get away with it.*

Struggling to my feet, I stumbled slowly to the pulpit. I drew in a deep breath, then exhaled quickly, sending a whistling wind into the microphone. The sound frightened me even more--and as I opened my mouth to begin speaking, to my dismay, nothing came out! *Nothing!* Sensing my loss for words, and realizing that he *had* to do something to salvage his high council image, Dad whispered the first words I had memorized. Taking this cue, I blurted, "Today I want to talk about faith and works. . . ."

Again my mind went blank, and again my father rescued me from certain ruin. "If we were in a rowboat," I repeated, suddenly and strangely gaining volume in my voice, "and had only one oar to row with, we would row in circles. However, when we have two oars, and use them at the same time, we can row directly to our destination."

Sensing I was on a roll, I continued without Dad's prompting, "So it is with faith and works. Each of these can be an oar. If we use only one, we'll travel in circles and go nowhere. If we use both faith and works at the same time, though, we'll be able to row ourselves all the way back to heaven. In the name of Jesus, Amen."

I knew I had memorized some other things about Joseph Smith and our new prophet, David O. McKay, but I didn't care. I knew the way out of my misery was in saying "Amen," so I did just that! Whirling around, I ran back to my seat and plunked myself down. I didn't dare look over at my dad; but as I sat down next to him, I immediately felt his arm reach around me. He hugged me tightly, and I glanced up out of the corner of my eye and smiled at him. He was one proud high councilor, I could tell that--perhaps the proudest high councilor in all the Church!

And me? Well, it had truthfully been the most frightening experience of my life. Still, I hadn't done too badly--even if I do say so myself. In fact, if I were totally truthful, I would have to say that, in a strange way I was looking forward to doing it again. After all, one day I might grow up to serve on the stake high council . . . just like my dad.

18

*A*wkward Moments

Startled, yet comforted by the realization that many years ago Heavenly Father began the preparation process for my service in the Mendon Ward--and feeling that Maria would receive compensating support--I came to myself sitting on the sofa with the old rowboat in my lap. I was strengthened knowing I would not be *alone* in this demanding phase of my life.

It seems that most large families have a menagerie of personality types among their children, and ours is no exception. First, we have vibrant and confident Walter, growing taller by the minute. Sarah is second, and is somewhat shy by nature. Her seemingly outwardly quiet personality disguises a fierce, competitive spirit that shows up both in school and in the wide variety of sports she participates in as a gifted athlete. Luke, on the other hand, seems blanketed with insecurities and does all within his power to please others. He possesses marvelous artistic skills and innately sees the relationships of colors and shapes. He began to draw at a very early age--and is becoming an artist with no small degree of talent. Luke also possesses a keen sensitivity to the feelings of others. Somehow he always knows who needs cheering up and how to do it. So his insecurities have always been a puzzle to me. There was a day, however, when the old treasure chest proved a source of help for both Luke *and* me.

One evening, when Maria was assisting at Girl's Camp, Luke informed me that he needed to talk about something in private. Naturally we went immediately to my den. Almost before the door closed, Luke began pouring out his heart about the little demons that he struggled with. He told me that he just wasn't going to be a good student like Walter and Sarah; nor would he ever succeed at sports, which came so naturally to both of them. He said that after *their* successes, he would just be a common ordinary son. He was most apologetic about his certain mediocre future.

"Now, Luke," I sighed, hopefully with the sage wisdom of an aging father, "don't draw conclusions about yourself too quickly. You don't get a final grade for life in elementary school. There's lots of time left, and you'll discover that some of the things that are important now will not be so important in the future."

Luke was quick to see the flaw in my logic, though, as he retorted, "That's great, Dad, but I don't *live* in the future. I live now, and I'm talking about how I feel today, not when I'm old like you and Mom. With my luck, I won't live to be that old, anyway."

"Okay . . . okay . . . ," I stammered, retreating as I spoke. "I have an idea, Luke. Let's go in the other direction and look into the past. What would you say to that?"

Luke's enthusiastic response surprised me, as he said, "That's what I hoped you'd say, Dad. I knew there would be something in the treasure box. So, what is it?"

To be honest, I wasn't sure what I might find, but I dutifully opened the lid to the chest and peered down among its contents. And as I did, my eyes fixed on a sturdy looking, little log house built of matches and popsicle sticks.

Gently, I revealed this priceless reminder of who *I* was, and who I was to become. As I started telling Luke the story of the little house, he become as emotionally involved as if he had been there himself the day it was completed. . . .

19

*M*atchsticks and Mansions

From the Eyes of a Sloth

"Ricky," Ted directed in exasperation, "will you please stop your day dreaming, and pass the mashed potatoes?!"

Pass, I thought, *that's easy for him to say--the guy that can throw a football in a perfect spiral for almost fifty yards. With my ability, if I tried to pass him the potatoes, I'd either throw it short and hit the water pitcher, or I'd overthrow him and cover our dog Conrad with a blanket of sticky white goo. Now, that would be interesting!*

Looking in the direction of our family dog, I could see him sitting there, unconcerned about his imminent mashed potato bath. Thinking of such a possible outcome brought a grin to my face, and for a moment I even considered "passing the potatoes" in Ted's direction. Good judgment won out, however, and I merely slid the bowl across our polished oak dining table. Even then, I was careful not to put too much force behind the dish.

Having completed my assignment, I immediately went back to my so-called daydream. *Why was I destined to be the only nerd in a family of athletes?* I could just see my children. They'd all be walking around the house bumping into things and spending days at the local hospital emergency room getting repaired.

At school it was the same thing. Boys my age were expected to be the harmonious extension of any athletic equipment we picked up. Footballs, basketballs, baseballs were supposed to be our best friends. But I didn't have talent at *anything:* sports, art, and music were all mysteries to me. In fact, besides feeling inferior in a family of jocks and artists, I frequently found myself envying the ability of some of my friends to do anything they tried. Whether it were sports, music, art, or schoolwork, these friends were able to excel with ease. It just came naturally to them.

I especially envied Randall Tenney. When it came to doing anything that required coordination, Randall beat everyone else without even trying. On the other hand, if you threw it, caught it, hit it, or ran with it, I *avoided* it. But not Randall--no, sireee! He could to do all these activities with the grace of a gazelle, the speed of a cheetah, and the cunning of a tiger.

For me, it was just the opposite. I was clearly at the bottom of the food chain when it came to eye-hand coordination. In fact, the infamous sloth comes to mind when thinking of an animal that describes my athletic skills. It is not a well-known fact that the sloth has superior intellectual skills, and it is not likely to become well-known. Such is the plight of the sloths. As they say, give a sloth a name and he'll live *down* to it!

Why, not long ago I even spent a full evening in the library down on Center Street studying sloths. Surprisingly, I found that they are actually very intelligent and handsome animals. After completing my research, I was prepared for lengthy discussions about what I had discovered. No one wanted to talk with me about sloths, though, because they'd rather talk about Randall Tenney.

My apparent lack of eye-hand coordination spilled over

81

into any project that required something to be made by hand. Anytime I went into a class and the teacher said something like "Boys and girls, today we are going to have a lot of fun; we are going to build something," I knew I was in trouble. Any sentence that started with *build* and included my involvement struck terror in the heart of this Primary-aged sloth.

I think things all came to a head that day. I journeyed through our cow pasture, down the steep gully, and over to Sister Hamlin's house. I was on my way to my very first Guide Patrol class activity. Seems harmless enough, right? Not so for me . . .

I was soon sitting with members of my patrol around a large, black, pot-bellied stove. Standing before us was our beautiful but aging teacher, Sister Hamlin. After all, the word was out that she was nearing her fortieth birthday. Her instructions were fairly simple, but frightening to the sloth. (That's *me,* in case you haven't been paying attention!) "Today, boys, we will be *building* something that will help us think about how our lives might turn out."

If the word "build" didn't make my heart stop, the rest of the sentence had been unwittingly designed to make me want to call in sick. But I was already there, so I just allowed things to unfold as they would. Nonetheless, I was certain that if I had to *build* something that would illustrate how my life was to turn out, I was in *BIG TROUBLE!*

While I was pondering my certain fate, Sister Hamlin handed each of us a large, new box of wooden matches. So far so good. In fact, I marveled at receiving my own full box of matches. *I've had matches taken away from me my entire life. Maybe this will be fun, after all!*

I didn't have long to consider this situation, however, before my curiosity was satisfied and, in fact, I developed a state of emotional paralysis. We were each given a paring knife and instructed to cut the heads off every match in our boxes. With every passing moment, this was looking more and more like a serious building project, and it was clear that things were *not* looking good for me.

We were the each given a large bottle of glue. "You will need the glue," Sister Hamlin said, confirming my greatest fears, "to *build* your own matchstick house. I have a cardboard base for each of you, and you may use this base to design and then build your very own log cabin. Your logs are obviously quite small, but *think* big, and you'll be excited to see your cabin take shape."

Having received our instructions, we immediately began to lay the matches out on our board, then shape them into a semblance of a log cabin. One by one, the matches were stacked on top of each other, then glued and held while the drying process began. As we worked, Sister Hamlin seemed literally to float amongst us, trying to get each of us started without mishap. Truthfully, it would have been a major undertaking for her to make my effort resemble anything other than a tilting haystack. In fact, some of the boys started snickering as they noticed my very feeble attempt at cabin building.

As I mentioned, I had just been advanced into the Guide Patrol, and it wasn't until later that I learned that when a new boy comes in, there is often a price for him to pay. The price wasn't meant to be personal; it was just tradition. But during that afternoon at Sister Hamlin's, I just thought it was me. You know, the sloth makes his first appearance in the Guide Patrol. . . .

Continuing as if she hadn't noticed the snickering, Sister Hamlin added, "You will discover, boys, that each matchstick, or log, must be placed carefully on top of the one below it. These tiny logs represent each day of your life. If you concentrate and place them with care, your cabin will become one of strength and endurance. On the other hand, if you are careless with any given log--or *day*--you will begin to create an unstable foundation that will impact you for the rest of your life."

Listening to Sister Hamlin's description of our assignment to build this house as a representation of our lives, I began to think about what I knew about sloths. I remembered two important points: the first, as you may recall, was that sloths were extremely handsome animals--if only to other sloths. However, I also remembered that they were quite intelligent. In my case, being handsome didn't seem to be useful in solving the building problem, so I decided that I would have to use some of my raw, native intellect to get out of this fix.

While I was pondering a variety of intellectual solutions, such as faking a heart attack or needing to go home and do my chores, Sister Hamlin broke the silence and announced, "Now, boys, I want you all to put your log cabins on the floor behind the stove. I know they aren't quite finished, but you need to understand *how* they are to be finished before you continue."

" *Finished?*" I muttered under my breath. "The only thing about to be finished is *me!*"

Not hearing my whispering, Sister Hamlin continued, "I haven't yet given you the lumber for your roofs because I need you to help me dry this lumber out."

Swinging around, she hastily retreated to her kitchen. We next heard the refrigerator door slam, and we knowingly grinned at each other. Sister Hamlin was famous for treats; in fact, going to her home on Halloween was always a highlight for us. She delighted in feeding growing boys. We weren't disappointed now, either. Before we knew it, she had returned, carrying a large sack of popsicles in a variety of colors.

"I've been eating popsicles for weeks now," she beamed, "just to save the sticks. I *have* saved quite a few, as you can imagine. But I need help if we're going to be ready for next Wednesday's roof building activity. Therefore, I'm giving each of you two *whole* popsicles. If you can't eat two of them, I'll understand. Just wash what you can't eat down the kitchen sink, then put the sticks on the drying tray. I'll have them cleaned and dried for next week's activity."

Two whole popsicles?!! I couldn't remember ever getting *one* whole popsicle to eat, let alone two! Why, as far as popsicles at my house were concerned, splitting one in half was the order of the day. Being the sixth of eight children, I knew well the maxim, "If you snooze, you lose!" I also knew that the cherry red ones, my favorite, would go fast. So I boldly jumped up and held out my hands. After all, even a sloth can move quickly when cherry popsicles are on the line--

"Why Richard," Sister Hamlin said kindly, "I'm so glad you want to help. You must know, however, that the Scout assisting always gets his choice last. But that's okay, because I'm sure you want your friends all to have their favorite flavors."

I was suddenly crestfallen as Sister Hamlin's words rang unexpectedly in my ears, and my heart fell all the way into my stomach, where only moments before I had expected two cherry red popsicles to land. In my eagerness, I had lost out--for I was certain that, just like me, all my friends liked the cherry red ones best. I knew it; they knew it, and within minutes of my jumping to my feet, I was standing alone, holding two lime green popsicles as if they were deadly germs.

Well, I sat there trying to act excited about the first lime green popsicle. Knowing I had to do something, I reluctantly began to break it in half. But Sister Hamlin must have had eyes in the back of her head, because before I knew it, she had left the room and returned--carrying two banana yellow popsicles. Now, everyone knows that banana yellow popsicles are really the very best, but are also quite rare.

"Here, Richard," she smiled, holding out the two extra popsicles. "I had these other two popsicles in my freezer. If you don't mind, the lime green ones are my very favorite. Would you feel badly if you traded with me?"

"Uh, sure . . ." I swallowed quickly, trying not to show too much excitement, "I'd be glad to."

"Thank you, Richard. It was nice of you to help me--and to be so generous in letting your friends choose first."

Her words had no sooner left her mouth than I immediately become the most popular boy in the room. *Everyone* wanted to trade. Pretty soon I had three whole cherry red popsicles and Randall Tenney, the sleek gazelle himself was kneeling on the floor showing me how to make my tilting haystack into a mansion.

As I said, sloths are among the most intelligent creatures in the entire animal kingdom--although it doesn't hurt to have an aging, wise owl for a Primary teacher.

Later that night, after all my family members had gone to bed, I sat very grown-up at my small bedroom desk. My lamp overhead was shining brightly, and my fingers were fumbling with a newly sharpened pencil. The sheet of paper in front of me was blank, except for a mark I had mistakenly made in the upper right-hand corner. Ignoring it, however, I slowly leaned forward and began to write:

Dear Sister Hamlin,

I came home today and got an idea. It's about the popsicle roofs. I think it would be good if you were to tell us that each popsicle stick is like one of the commandments. If we place them over our lives--for protection--they can keep us dry and warm, even if the weather outside is awful!

Don't tell the other boys I suggested this. They would just think I was showing off or something. Oh, and thanks for the banana popsicles! I'm sure you don't know this, but banana is my favorite flavor. It is my friends' favorite, too, so I hope I didn't offend you when I traded for their cherry reds.

Good luck,
RICHARD

Placing the note inside a small envelope, I placed it carefully on the edge of my desk so I would remember to mail it in the morning.

Then, following a quick prayer, I hopped into bed and began dreaming about myself as the wisest sloth in the neighborhood. I could see my future clearly--the father of a large family of beautiful and intelligent sloths. Things looked better than they had for a long time, and I was sure that next week I would bring home a perfect mansion of matches and popsicle sticks.

20

*T*he Tide
Begins To Turn

"Gee, Dad," Luke interjected suddenly, bringing us right back into the peaceful confines of my study, "I didn't know you were a nerd like me. I thought you were an all-star basketball player in high school. Did you just make that story up, or something, to make me feel better?"

"No, Son," I responded with a knowing smile, "even sloths become interesting to coaches when they stand six-and-a-half feet tall. Furthermore, sloths can do a lot with a basketball when they practice every night after school from age 14 on."

"Oh yeah, right!" Luke retorted with obvious sarcasm. "But, what does that have to do with me? I'm not tall, and no coach has ever even noticed me--at least not for my athletic potential. Though there was the time I fell from the climbing rope during PE, and everyone thought I was dead. That day I was the most noticed boy at school, believe me!"

"Now, come on, Luke," I said, trying to give him a little reassurance. "Aren't you the tallest boy in your grade?"

"Yeah, sure . . . But, what good does *that* do? About the

only benefit at school is that I get to help Mrs. Shipley change the multiplication cards that she lines up across the top of the blackboard."

"Well, Luke, I can only say that time will reveal the advantages of your being the tallest in your grade. The charts at the doctor's office predict that you'll be two inches taller than I am by the time you finish growing. This will probably make you the tallest in this family, as well as in your high school."

"Okay, Dad," Luke countered. "Suppose that's true . . . so *what*?"

"That's a very good question." I then held the match and popsicle-stick mansion out to him. "And the answer is found right here."

As he took the small log cabin from me, I added, "What really matters, Luke, is what you're building as time goes on. It's not what awards you earn for being tall. After all, who would have thought a sloth could have come up with such a magnificent piece of work as this little house?" I then winked mischievously. "As I've been telling you," I continued, "it all came about because of a sloth's good looks and intelligence!"

"Well, Dad, if there are still a lot of possibilities ahead, maybe I can look forward to my *own* adventures as a sloth. Thanks for listening. . . ."

Luke then got up and started to leave the room--but not without a hug from me. I could tell from the sound of his footsteps that he really *did* feel better about himself and his future. As for me, I stayed awhile in my study. I wanted to determine how I could introduce the "sloth concept" to Maria without her feeling patronized. In addition, I had noticed something in my treasure chest that bothered me, and I wanted to take a closer look.

Settling into my recliner, I pulled the box closer and reopened it. After carefully putting my miniature stick mansion back into its compartment, I slowly examined the other articles in sight. Just as I thought. There were only three items left that had not previously been seen by my family.

As I looked at these three remaining treasures, I realized that they all had something in common. I had received each memento after an experience in my life that taught me more about the Savior and what he did for us. Pondering this fact gave me a real sense of anticipation, as I looked forward to teaching my family about Christ.

Not more than three weeks later, after an especially long Sunday at the bishop's office, I came into the house looking and *feeling* exhausted. After all those years, Maria seemed to know my moods even better than I did and greeted me with, "Hi, honey, you look tired, so you must have had a busy day. Why don't you go on up to your study and relax? I'll send one of the kids up to get you when dinner is ready."

Without resistance, I silently wandered through the house toward the stairs to my study. I wanted to say *hello* to the kids, but I ended up saying nothing. Those I could find weren't all that interested in me--after all, it was only Dad-- so I simply trudged up the stairs. I had no sooner found my way into my study and removed my shoes, than Maria arrived at the door with a warm plate of Sunday dinner. *Surely,* I considered, *microwaves were invented for bishops!*

Knowing that I needed time to unwind, Maria gave me a peck on the cheek and told me she'd be up later to visit. I was feeling grateful for her sensitivity, and thought that perhaps reviewing my matchstick mansion experience with Luke would be an easy way for Maria to learn from it, as well. Considering this possibility, I slowly ate my meal.

Minutes later, Maria was in the room, and before I knew it, the two of us were examining the small matchstick mansion. I was also sharing my conversation with Luke, and although she didn't respond verbally, I could see that the story was having an impact on her, as well. When I concluded, and we finished talking about Luke and what he had learned, Maria quietly excused herself. I could see that she needed to be alone to process what I had shown her, so I remained quiet as she retreated from the room. It was several days before I learned that introducing the small cabin to Maria did not have the effect I had hoped for.

But for now, feeling naively good with how our discussion had gone, I dismissed the small cabin from my mind and began mentally to review the events of the day.

One particularly sweet interview I'd held had helped a couple in the ward increase their understanding of the nature of repentance and of the Savior's atoning sacrifice. This thought spun into another, and I soon found myself wondering when *I* had actually begun to develop an understanding of the Savior's love. That's when I again thought of the chest.

Opening the box back up, I pulled out an old, leather dog collar. Remembering where this collar came from, I just as quickly placed it back inside the box. I then waited until Family Home Evening the following night so I could introduce it to my family.

The day passed, and soon it was my turn to give the lesson. Gathering my family around me, I conveniently pulled out the leather dog collar. Immediately, as I began to envision my closest childhood friend, my family joined me in remembering. Although I knew they had heard some of the stories before, I also sensed that hearing them again in the confines of my office would give added insight. Once again, the distances of time seemed to melt away as I began to tell them of the former owner of the leather collar. It took only a brief introduction. . . .

21

The Greatest Love

of All

As our new, big-finned 1955 Plymouth moved slowly out of the Church parking lot, I stared out into space. With some urging from my mother about what was on my mind, I finally responded with, "Mom, I just don't understand that scripture, and I don't think I ever will."

"Well, Ricky," she replied softly, "we can look up the verses when we get home, and then I'll see if I can help you."

Now, that was a mistake, I realized. *It's only five o'clock in the afternoon. With little more than an hour until dinner time, I had planned to go outside and play with my friends. But not today! No, I'm going to be studying the scriptures. I should have kept my thoughts to myself!*

Well, that was how that particular afternoon went. With Mom's help, I looked up the scripture. We found it in John 15:13, and I read aloud: "Greater love hath no man than this, that a man lay down his life for his friends. . . ."

"Mom," I sighed, "I just don't get it. Why did Jesus have to die? Couldn't Heavenly Father have thought of an easier way for Jesus to pay for our sins? After all, isn't He the most powerful person in the universe?"

While we were talking, the moments dragged slowly on. Mom tried to help me understand, but I just couldn't see it. I knew that Jesus' mother, Mary, must have felt just awful when her special Son died such a horrible death, and I didn't understand why it had to be so painful.

Our suppertime conversation centered on this topic, and Dad talked a long time about some things I didn't understand. For example, he tried to explain that sometimes there are things we can't do for ourselves, and someone who *really* loves us would give up everything of value to help. I kept nodding like I understood what he was saying, but in truth it just didn't make sense. Usually, my dad was a good explainer, but tonight he was a little off his game.

He brought the discussion to a close by saying, "Now, Ricky, does that help?"

Not wanting to prolong the conversation, I simply acknowledged that it did. Pretty soon we were all picking up the dishes and taking them into the kitchen. After rinsing mine off, I went on up to my room to finish my homework. Though such a scene might look good to the casual observer, this was not a typical evening at our house. Frequently I came in late for dinner because I stayed out playing too long. Sometimes I didn't go up and finish my homework, and I hardly *ever* picked up the dinner dishes. But tonight was different. Maybe it was because of that scripture; I don't know. Eventually, though, I went to bed without getting it all sorted out.

By the next day at the bus stop, I had forgotten about the scripture in the Bible. In fact, I didn't think about again it for several months. It came to mind again in midsummer, though, while we were vacationing at Meteor Lake. Dad had rented a cabin for two weeks, including the Fourth of July holiday. Even though he planned to go back down to work on Wednesdays and Thursdays, we still got him for most of the time. It was going to be a great vacation.

The best part was that my folks let me bring my dog, Conrad--which, for me, meant that I would be bringing my best friend. In our preparation, we loaded all our stuff into the station wagon, then the others rode up to the Lake with Mom in her blue car. Conrad and I rode with Dad, because Conrad had to ride in the station wagon. It was an Allred family rule: No dogs in Mom's car.

It was comforting to have such a pet for a best friend. Conrad was huge, exceptionally friendly, and maybe the smartest member of the family. After all, everyone knew he liked me best.

After we arrived at the Lake, Conrad and I were sitting near the shore when I began thinking about how good it was to have such a faithful, loyal friend. Then I remembered the scripture in John, and I realized that it still didn't make sense. I just didn't think it was necessary for friends to show the importance of their friendship by giving up their life. I knew Conrad loved me without *that*. Besides, how can you still be friends if one of you is gone?

As I was thinking about all of this, I started reviewing several episodes in Conrad's life that had cemented our friendship. I remembered that it wasn't too long after Conrad arrived and got a little growth that it became apparent that everyone in our neighborhood really liked him--including the adults. He was so friendly, in fact, that some mothers brought their dog-shy children over to our house to help them overcome their fear of big animals. Conrad never disappointed them, either. I could clearly visualize these little kids as they tugged at his ears, got on his back, and even pulled his tail. And all he would do was wag his tail and lick their faces with his gigantic slobbery tongue.

The night we were given Conrad as a baby puppy, we got together as a family to decide what his name should be. Because he was to be *my* puppy, it was really my choice, but I couldn't think of a good name. Dad said he had the potential of becoming a great host, just like Conrad Hilton, so we decided to call him Conrad. The name stuck, although we eventually changed it to Conrad Allred just to help him feel more like part of the family.

I don't know how it first happened, but I have clear memories of Conrad following me to Primary on Wednesday afternoons. And even though he couldn't come inside the chapel, he somehow figured out which classroom I was in. He must have seen me through the open window, because he would lie down outside that very window taking in all that I was learning.

I'm sure that being able to attend class, even from outside on the grass, was the thing that made Conrad such an unusual animal. He attended as regularly as I did, yet never made a sound. I think he somehow knew that if my teacher, Sister Hamlin, discovered that he was there, she might have chased him off. She didn't ever seem to see him, though, nor did my classmates. Things always seemed to have a way of working out for the best.

When these scenes of Conrad's early life passed from view, I found myself at the lake, lying by the edge of the water, looking up into the sky. I began thinking about how Conrad had slowly become a legend in our neighborhood. There was the time he climbed almost eight feet up a tree, then gently took Mary Robert's kitten by the back of its neck, between his teeth, and jumped down. That adventuresome kitten got stuck up in the tree and was whining at a fever pitch, but none of us boys could climb such a tall tree. So Conrad, sensing the problem, simply crawled up there and solved it.

Now, people have said that dogs don't climb trees, and I understand how they might doubt Conrad's response to such an emergency. But you can see for yourself. We've got pictures in our scrapbook to prove it! As it turned out, when Mom heard the ruckus, she looked out the window just as Conrad was making his way up the tree. She ran and got the camera, so we have pictures for all the world to see.

Then there was the time the burglar came. One night

when Dad was out of town, we heard some strange sounds coming from the mud room by the back door. We had just turned out the lights on our way up to bed. No one wanted to go downstairs alone, but somehow I was chosen to go down with Mom. Without turning the lights back on, we sneaked down the stairs where we saw a shadow moving through the back door window. Then noises came from the back door that sounded like someone was trying to break into the house.

These sounds were followed by a terrible growling and barking sound. Now it was Conrad's custom to sleep out on the patio beneath the chair swing. We always marveled that he could even sleep through a thunderstorm. At this moment, though, he must have sensed that something was terribly wrong. All of the sudden there was a horrendous amount of noise coming from a dog that never barked at *anything or anyone*! As we looked out the window, we saw a shadowy figure run from the house and jump over the back fence with Conrad in hot pursuit!

Seeing we were out of danger, Mom had the presence of mind to call for help. Within a very few minutes, we heard police sirens down the street. Not very long after that, a knock came at our front door. It was Officer Wilhelm from the police department. And would you believe it? Standing beside him, with a little grin on his face, was Conrad. Everyone in town seemed to know Conrad, so it was no surprise that Officer Wilhelm knew where to bring him.

Now I don't know if normal dogs can act pleased, but this was Conrad, and he sure seemed proud of what he had done. Officer Wilhelm told us that without Conrad's help, they probably wouldn't have caught the man. Our usually friendly dog had chased the burglar, while barking up a storm, until the police caught up with them. All of Conrad's barking and growling had led the police right to the villain. As it turned out, the man was a stranger just passing through town. He had burglarized at least three other houses before the police caught up with him.

Looking back, this was one of the incidents Dad had used when he we talked about the scripture in John about friends giving their all for friends. Dad said there are some things we just can't do for ourselves, and true friends will stick their necks all the way out for us. Then he reminded me that Conrad had come completely out of character that night, simply because he seemed to know that this was the only way he could help us.

After the incident with the burglar, Conrad truly did become one of the family. This "adoption" was not without adjustments, however. For a while, Mom had insisted that he not be fed table scraps. She also had a rule that we couldn't feed him from our plate while *we* were eating. The problem wasn't just with us kids, either. Sometimes when we weren't having company, Dad let Conrad put his front paws up on the table and eat right off his plate. It was usually the food Dad wouldn't eat, like asparagus or Brussels sprouts, but it *was* on Mom's list of food that was good for us. We all wondered what the big deal was; after all Conrad *would become* healthier, wouldn't he?

I suppose Mom passed the "no scraps rule" in exasperation, and we all tried to obediently follow it--sort of. Eventually that rule, and others like it, fell apart. Usually these rules broke down because one of us would catch Mom breaking them--like slipping Conrad a morsel or two with her left hand underneath the table cloth when she thought no one was looking. One night, when we caught her doing this, everyone laughed and the rule was immediately tossed out the window. From that day forward, Conrad started eating with us almost every evening. It just seemed as if he were one of us.

For some reason, I kept seeing all these old Conrad incidents floating through my mind with him sitting next to me, while the wind-driven waves of Meteor Lake pushed up against our bare feet. In truth, there were *hundreds* of Conrad stories, and within minutes another came into my mind.

When my sister Mary Ellen was about five years old, she had a goldfish that she kept in a small, round fish bowl in her bedroom. One day, as she later admitted, she was dipping her hands in the water, trying to catch that fish. Conrad was lying on the floor nearby, watching with minimum interest. *After all*, he likely thought, *what was so exciting about a goldfish?*

Well, anyway, Mary Ellen couldn't catch the fish. As a final attempt, she cupped both hands together and put them deep into the bowl. Drawing her hands out of the bowl, she managed to capture the goldfish and lift it out of the water.

Instead of being proud of her success, however, Mary Ellen panicked when the fish started flopping around in her hands. In shock, she opened her hands and dropped it. Conrad, who had likely fallen asleep, suddenly found himself taking an unexpected shower. He awakened with a start when the goldfish landed right on his nose, then bounced to the carpeted floor. As you would expect, the fish then began flopping around, and Mary Ellen started screaming at the top of her lungs.

At that moment, Conrad did the craziest thing--*he ate the fish*! He just opened his mouth, stuck out his tongue, and effortlessly lapped it up. Needless to say, the fish's disappearing act didn't set all that well with Mary Ellen. She immediately lost it. Picking up her fish bowl as evidence, she increased the volume on her panic generator and ran to find Mom. Conrad just nonchalantly trotted along behind her.

Mary Ellen was in a total frenzy when she finally found Mom. Taking the fish bowl and placing it safely on the floor, Mom calmed Mary Ellen down and asked her what had happened. After hearing a tear-filled explanation of the fish's last moment on earth, Mom turned to fuss at Conrad, who at that very moment was just entering the room. Now, no one minded Conrad getting the scraps--but *not* the goldfish. It just wasn't right.

Raising her voice, she exclaimed, *"Conrad*, what have

you done with Mary Ellen's fish?!!"

Without even breaking stride, Conrad trotted over to the fish bowl. Then, opening his mouth, as if to lap up a drink, he surprisingly revealed the fish, still alive, wiggling frantically on his tongue. Who knows what the fish was thinking at that moment? Probably about Jonah and the whale, if fish think about such things. In a split second, Conrad somehow spit that fish down into the bowl, then backed up and sat on his haunches, as if to admire his feat. The fish lay momentarily on its side, then slowly started swimming around, no doubt comforted at being back in familiar territory.

Conrad, meanwhile, seemed unaffected by it all. But _we_ wondered how he always seemed to be there when we needed him and then seemed to know exactly how to help.

Anytime we share Conrad stories, people often seem to doubt them . . . at least _until_ they meet Conrad. But you don't have to be around that dog very long before you believe any story you hear about him.

As Conrad and I lay there by the side of the lake, I continued dreaming about many other experiences we'd shared. These quiet thoughts heightened my excitement to be up at the cabin with my best friend, Conrad Hilton Allred.

We had a blast that summer; with every day a new adventure! Why, one night Mom even let Conrad and me sleep out under the stars. She would have never let me sleep outside alone, but she knew I was safe with Conrad sleeping next to me.

Early the next morning, after a night outdoors, Conrad and I decided to go up to the other side of the lake to watch the sunrise. Little did I know, when the two of us awakened, that by the end of the day I would have a much better understanding of the meaning of the nearly forgotten scripture in _John_ about friendship.

It was approaching first light when we left the cabin, and I knew we'd have to hurry to make it. So I violated one of the *Allred Rules of the Woods*. Instead of following along the safe trail to the edge of the lake as the rule demanded, I took the shortcut across Cranberry Ridge. We then ran down the steep side of Carrington's Bluff. The last two hundred yards or so included crossing the logging road twice, and that was *the* problem. In fact, another of the *Allred Rules of the Woods* stated that we never cross over the logging road without Mom or Dad--not even when we were with Conrad.

The reason for the rule was obvious to those who knew anything about the geography around Meteor Lake. There was a major logging company located up the mountain, not too far from our cabin. Logging trucks came down the mountain road going awfully fast, and making the turn near Carrington's Bluff was the hardest part of the trip. The grade was very steep, and sometimes, if the driver had a full load of timber, he could barely retain control of the rig.

But on this morning, with little concern, Conrad and I hurried along the less-traveled trail, crossing over Cranberry Ridge. Without our knowing it, however, at almost that very same minute, one of those logging trucks was beginning its descent. Since it was early in the morning, the driver didn't want to awaken anyone, so he didn't sound his usual warning horn at strategic points during his descent. Besides, as he later explained, he couldn't imagine that anyone, let alone a boy and a dog, would possibly be on the road at 5:30 in the morning.

As Conrad and I approached the edge of the road at the first switchback, we just dashed across. We then quickly moved up the trail to the top of Carrington's Bluff and came to the second crossing. This one was much more difficult than the first, however, because we had to enter the road from a fairly steep embankment about fifteen feet above the roadway. There was no way to avoid sliding as we worked our way down toward the road.

Adding to the danger was the curve in the road that kept the trucks from view until they arrived at the second crossing. And further, no truck driver could see hikers coming out of the woods--that is, until it was, plain and simply, too late. . . .

At the time we arrived at the second crossing, Conrad was several yards behind me. As I started down the embankment, I turned, whistled for him, and heard his bark. But looking back for Conrad unexpectedly caused me to lose my footing, and I slid quickly down onto the roadway.

At that very second, the logging truck came barreling around the bend. Because of its heavy load, the truck was going too fast. When the driver saw me, it was too late for him to effectively apply his brakes. He honked to warn me, but that didn't help, as I was already tumbling out onto the road. When I realized what was happening, I froze--

I think I may have closed my eyes, because I honestly didn't see what happened next. I only felt something slam into my back, knock the wind out of me, and send me flying to the edge of the steep drop-off on the far side of the road. As you may have guessed, the blow I felt was Conrad, who apparently jumped from the hillside above and behind me! He hit me *so* hard that he pushed me completely across the road--and thereby saved my life.

But poor Conrad! He bounced onto the road so hard that the impact completely knocked the wind out of him. So, there he lay--unable to move--in the direct path of the oncoming truck.

The driver later explained that he swerved to try to avoid my path as I was thrown across the road. In doing so, this impulse maneuver caused his truck to head straight toward Conrad. As I slid into the bank on the far side of the road, I looked back in time to see the truck run right over the spot where Conrad lay. Gratefully, I didn't hear so much as a whimper from my best friend.

In seconds it was all over. The truck went some distance down the road before it stopped. In shock, I ran back toward Conrad's lifeless body. For some reason, the scripture flashed back into my mind right there as I was running back toward Conrad. Although I couldn't quote it perfectly, I did think, *"Greater love hath no man . . . that he lay down his life for his friend. . . ."*

"Oh, no!" I screamed frantically. "It *can't* be!!"

As I got closer, I realized that there wasn't any visible blood. Even so, I could see tire tracks and skid marks all over the dirt road. With a glimmer of hope, I rushed directly to Conrad and threw myself down beside him. However, as I pulled his lifeless head into my lap, I knew for certain what had happened. Today I had truly lost my best friend. I buried my head into his fur and released a grief-filled cry that came from somewhere deep within me.

For a moment I felt a rush of anger inside of me that was greater than any I had ever experienced. I was mad at the truck driver, whom I could see running down the road toward us. I was upset with myself for not being more careful. *Why did this have to turn out this way,* I fumed? *It just isn't fair.* I guess I felt angry at the whole world.

Then I lifted my head up and looked down once again at my dear, caring, now lifeless friend. I realized right then that I wasn't angry with Conrad. In fact, I felt a wave of love for him that more than eclipsed my anger. I was filled with a wonderfully warm feeling that seemed very strange, given the circumstances. That's when the scripture from *John* again came back into mind.

Even though I was young and didn't fully understand my feelings, I did have a sense of a deeper truth. I loved Conrad more right then than I had ever loved him. I believed then, and still do, that he sensed the risk when he leaped off the side of the hill to save my life. If it were him or me, he chose to stand in for me and suffer all the consequences of my foolish decisions. Though I didn't know it then, in this moment of great anguish, I was beginning to understand what Christ meant when he said, "Greater love hath no man than this, that a man lay down his life for his friends. . . ."

22

*P*aying the Price

As the vision of Conrad and Meteor Lake mysteriously faded from view, I found myself holding the dog collar in an almost reverential way. Looking up at my family, I could see that they also had been touched by the scene along the road near the lake, for some were very quiet and others were sniffling. Then one of the children broke the spell by asking, "Dad, I thought that Conrad was your good friend right through high school. Don't I remember some stories about him later in your life?"

"That's right," I agreed, "but the lesson learned was not affected by his recovery. It wasn't until the truck driver came up and used some basic first aid on Conrad that he started breathing again. Though he was seriously injured, he recovered by the end of the summer and lived many more years, providing us with lots of additional Conrad stories. However, from that day forward I saw Conrad in a new light. My sense of closeness to him remained until his last day on earth. Today it is clear to me that many simple

103

things of my early life helped build a foundation for my understanding of Christ's love for his friends, including me."

Though they didn't say much as they filtered out of the room toward the kitchen and refreshments, I could tell that my children had learned new ideas from hearing the story told under the influence of the old treasure chest. As the others were leaving, I noticed that Walter was lingering cautiously behind. What he did next directly altered the spirit of the evening. I should mention that I knew that this was a time in his life when Walter was experiencing the typical joys and frustrations of being a teenager. So it came as no real surprise when broke into my thoughts with an outburst: "It's not fair, Dad! No one has ever done it for me, and I don't think I should have to continue to do it for them!"

Taking a deep breath, I tried to bring myself all the way into Walter's concerns, although I have to admit, it wasn't easy. "Now, Walter," I sighed, "what's going on?"

"Well," he snapped, "you know all about it. It was your rule in the first place, and I don't think it's *fair!*"

"Which rule is that, Son?" I asked patiently, knowing that he deserved the same gracious treatment as those who come to see me in the bishop's office. Even so, to show Walter the same caring response that I managed at Church seemed to be a Herculean task. After all, it had been a long day, and I felt that he was really breaking up the tender feelings I'd been having as I remembered my childhood friend, Conrad. I probably just needed to be alone. No such luck, however.

Walter continued, hardly taking a breath, "You know the rule: Walter is the oldest. That makes him protector, best friend, and companion to all his siblings. It doesn't matter that he has other plans. No sireee! Whatever the younger kids need, Walter is Johnny-on-the-spot to serve them until time is concluded--or until the millennium begins, whichever comes first! Frankly, Dad, I'm just getting tired of it!"

I knew this wasn't the time to discuss the folly of exaggeration. I didn't think it would play well to Walter in his current state of mind, although I considered it as an attempt to soften his distress. Then I thought better of it. Showing outward patience, while waiting for my emotions to catch up with my resolve, I asked, "Now Son, what seems to be causing all this stress? Right now, today, I mean."

"Well, tomorrow night for mutual we are having a combined stake activity and everyone is going. But I *can't* go. I have a report due next Friday, and I need to get started on it. Tom Wilson from school is coming over and we were going to get a jump on the whole thing. But Mom says I need to take Sarah because she can't drive. Why is it always me?"

"Well, I can see your point," I responded, really trying to see his point.

"Can you, Dad? I don't think so. Mom said I should come up to talk with you, but I knew what you'd say before I got here. You'd listen in your calm understanding way, then point out how a mature person should act. Then I'd feel guilty and have to take Sarah to the fireside anyway. Plus I would end up talking Tom into coming with us, and everything would be just fine--that is, until the next time. Dad, when does this stop? I'm getting tired of being told that I'm the oldest, and that it goes with the territory. It looks like a bad real estate deal to me."

All of that came out of Walter in almost a single breath. He went on to recount four or five times the previous week when he played tutor, chauffeur, counselor, and friend to his younger siblings. Generally, he added, these roles were played at times of great inconvenience to himself, and sometimes at great embarrassment.

It wasn't too late in the evening, and it was still 24 hours before the fireside. I knew that Walter really wanted to talk about this, so I settled down and just listened. Finally, in an effort to calm him down, I walked over to my treasure box, picked it up, and carried it over to the sofa.

"You know, Walter, I haven't allowed anyone to look into the box since we first started using it. However, because you're the oldest, I have an idea. Would you like to see inside?"

"Boy, would I!" he replied excitedly. Then, with a hint of a smile, he added, "But don't think you can bribe me into changing my mind."

Raising my hand, I promised him that it was not a bribe. Together we opened the box. For the first time Walter looked down inside and saw the different compartments. Some of them were open at the top, and others had lids on them that were connected by hasps and hinges to their particular partitions. The inside work was as professional and well-crafted as the outside and seemed to make a real impression on Walter.

"Gee, Dad, your uncle ValGene was a good carpenter, wasn't he?"

Nodding in agreement, then giving Walter time to take it all in, I carefully asked if I could share a story with him. Allowing him to be the first of the children to look inside the box must have gotten to him because his interest was obvious.

With that encouragement, I reached into the box and extracted a small picture of Christ. It was encased in a gold metal frame, and had been carefully wrapped in tissue paper. I remembered with immediate clarity the day my brother Ted gave it to me. The images that passed before my eyes were of a time only a few months before I was given this special picture. I wasn't very old--maybe six or seven--and I was playing outside with some friends. Even though I knew that Walter would quickly get into the story, I thought an introduction would be helpful, and so I began.

23

*W*hat's An

Older Brother For?

One summer, while playing the role of Superman in Caroline Vining's back yard, I was bitten by her family dog. It would be an understatement to say I was embarrassed as I was whisked away to the emergency room in the family car with Mom. At the time I was wearing an authentic Superman shirt which I'd gotten for a cereal box top and fifty cents. What added to my dismay was having to explain to the doctor how Superman could suffer a flesh wound while protecting the known universe. This otherwise unimportant episode left me afraid of dogs for a long time.

Throughout that summer there were other unfortunate incidents with antagonistic dogs. The most notable one included my older brother Ted. If ever there were a candidate for Super Hero, Ted was it. He was absolutely fearless--a mighty protector of little brothers in times of danger. As the one of his several little brothers most likely to get into trouble, it naturally fell upon my shoulders to become a beacon of his successes. There were no perils that seemed too treacherous for Ted. He was afraid of neither bullies nor bulldogs. In fact, ferocious, barking dogs were his specialty.

One day the two of us were walking home from Primary, when suddenly from out of nowhere, racing directly toward me, was an immense dog. It was probably the biggest dog in the universe! It was half-barking, half-growling, and intermittently baring its teeth. No shark was any better equipped to put the bite on a person. As this vicious and raging animal drew closer, I instantly realized that I was experiencing my last day on earth as a recognizable human being! So much for my career as a super hero!

Suddenly and without warning, Ted stepped between me and the beast. Still, the animal didn't slow down until he was about a bite away from Ted. Fearful of nothing, Ted stooped down so that his face was almost on the same level as the raging creature. Ted then let out the loudest growl I had ever heard. As he did, he moved his head from side to side and lunged toward the dog. Immediately, the mutt dropped its head, tucked its tail between its legs, and scampered back down the driveway.

What a breath-taking moment! When it was clearly over, Ted glanced down at me, noticing how surprised and grateful I appeared to be. He winked and continued to lead us along the sidewalk as though nothing out of the ordinary had transpired. I noticed that he kind of shuffled his feet along the sidewalk for a few steps when he was aware that I was staring at him, but other than that, he didn't say much at all.

As we continued walking down the street, I became increasingly proud of Ted. I asked him how he knew what to do. I also wanted to know how he got the courage up to pull off this bluff with the dog. Knowing to bark and growl was one thing, but standing there and *doing* it was clearly another. So I kept pressing Ted to tell me his secret.

For some time, he didn't answer. Instead, he just brushed it off as if it were nothing. He didn't act proud or anything; he just acted like he didn't want to talk about it. But I couldn't let it go. After all, it was one of the bravest acts of heroism I had ever seen--and he had done it for *me*!

Finally, after much pleading on my part, Ted looked down at me and said, "You know, Ricky, Mom and Dad have always told me to be your protector. It must have been the first thing they said to me after you came home from the hospital. I also heard it on your first day of school and on your first day at Primary. The typical message, whenever we did anything together was, 'Don't forget to take care of Ricky.' They even made me take you along when I went places with my friends. Quite honestly, I just got tired of it. I don't mean to hurt your feelings, but I haven't always wanted to be with you, let alone protect you. Sometimes I wanted just to be with my friends without you tagging along."

Now, Ted had never spoken like this, so I carefully asked, "Then, why did you get between me and that dog?"

"Well," he replied thoughtfully, "last year in Primary we had an Easter lesson that changed it all for me. I don't think Sister Noonschwander necessarily intended her message to have the effect it had on me, but I guess that happens with some lessons. Anyway, that day she told us about Jesus, who gave everything for *His* brothers and sisters. As a part of this special lesson, she gave each one of us a small picture of Christ in a gold frame. I had heard the story before, of course, but this time I heard it differently.

"I just couldn't help thinking: *My Older Brother did everything He could for me, His little brother, without complaining just because His Father asked.* Don't you see, Ricky, I had to do the same thing, in my own way, for *my* little brother?

"I don't always think of Christ as my older brother," Ted continued. "More often I remember Him as my Savior and Redeemer. Occasionally, however, thinking of Him as my older brother helps me a lot. And now, since that lesson, I honestly feel like it's a privilege--rather than a burden--to help *you* out.

"So when I saw that dog coming toward you, I knew I had to step in. Suddenly, from out of nowhere, a thought came into my mind: *Act like a dog.* At first I didn't get it, but then the thought came into my mind with greater detail, *Act like this dog.* That was when I got it.

"Without hesitating, I dropped to my knees, bared my teeth, and growled. Seconds later when that dog started whimpering and turned away, I almost laughed at the sight. But I didn't because I was afraid I'd break the spell."

After Ted finished his explanation, we didn't speak as resumed our journey. But I'll say this: I felt safe as we walked along. I just knew that with older brothers like Ted and Jesus I would always make it safely home.

24

With Christ
in the Picture

By the time I finished the story, Walter was holding the picture of Christ in his hands and was very quiet. I wasn't sure what he was thinking until he asked, "Dad, when you were telling that story, I could really visualize the scene. What's more, I had a very unusual impression. Dad, what *was* that feeling?"

"Why don't you describe it," I replied gently, "then maybe I can help you understand it?"

Immediately he struggled with words, "Well," he began "I'm not sure. It . . . well . . . I guess I would say it was a warm, peaceful feeling. . . ."

I had a difficult time speaking at first, knowing what had just happened to my oldest son. But, gathering myself together, I explained, "Well, Walter, the scriptures say that we will get a warm and peaceful feeling when the Lord is trying to talk with us through the Spirit. I suspect that's what happened to you."

"That's what I thought," he mused, and then put his head in his hands and said nothing.

I allowed the moment to linger until he was ready to reply. At last, speaking very slowly, he said, "I'm really surprised to find out that Heavenly Father is interested in *me*. I never realized that He was so concerned about my life and what I am doing. It makes me want to do better so I won't let Him down."

With that, he shot out of his chair. Although his sudden movement seemed a little abrupt, Walter was always one for making quick decisions when he could see the proper response. "You know, Dad, if I'm going to go to that fireside tomorrow night, I'd better call Tom and reschedule our study time."

As quickly as he finished his sentence, Walter bounded out of the room and down the stairs. And as he did, I placed the gold-framed picture back inside my chest. It was then that I noticed the last memento. It was a branch, really almost a twig, from an olive tree that I had been given many years ago in a Primary class. I felt certain it would not be long before this olive branch would have an impact on Maria, as well as on the rest of the family.

25

T*hough Your Sins*

Be As Scarlet

It was only a few evenings later that I walked into my study and found Maria sitting beside the sofa. The opened treasure chest was directly in front of her. She was so lost in thought that she didn't even realize that I had come into the room. As I silently observed her, I realized that she was quietly crying while holding several of the mementoes in her lap. I didn't want to interrupt this private moment, but I was too concerned about her to just walk away and leave her there alone. "Honey," I reluctantly asked, "are you okay?"

Wiping her eyes, while acting very embarrassed, she blurted out, "Okay? ...Am I okay? No, I'm *not* okay! And I wonder if I ever will be! If it hadn't been for this old chest, everything would be fine. But no, you had to dig it out of the attic and open up your 'never-never-land' past! I wish we'd just thrown it away when we moved here!"

To say I was shocked at her outburst would be an understatement. Trying somewhat to recover, I measured my words. "Wait a minute. . . . I thought the treasures in this old box had been useful in teaching things to our children."

"Teaching things?" she repeated in a mocking tone. "Oh, sure! Things from a mythical childhood that only happens to people like you and characters in story books. What about *my* life? Where are the treasured mementoes from my childhood that we could use to teach anything to the kids? You want mementoes, I'll show you some. Let's go back to that old county courthouse in Utah and get the divorce decree that the judge granted my father. Then I could show you some *real* lessons of life! I could tell the kids about a grown man who abandoned his eight-year-old daughter and her mother. Or, how about my years in the big city? Now, what could I use from that period to illustrate the ravages of sin?!"

With tremendous energy, Maria then tossed the keepsakes she'd been holding back into the box. In one motion she slammed down the lid, turned her face into one of the sofa pillows and began to sob uncontrollably. It was as though the pain of a lifetime of buried frustration, anger, and guilt surged through her in one defining moment. In truth, I was totally dumbfounded.

"Maria . . ." I finally gathered myself together enough to speak, "what can I say that can help? I just don't understand why--"

"You don't know *why*?!" she snapped back, incredulously. "How can it not be obvious to you? For some time now we've opened up the chest of your childhood to solve family problems. I'll admit that some of the illustrations were fun and interesting, and many times they provided a spiritual uplift even for me. But, as you know, there have been times when I've purposely stayed away from the discussions. This didn't help, though, because either you or the kids would always fill me in. . .just like with the matchstick house. Don't you *see*, Richard?! What became a magical box for you and the kids has become a *Pandora's box* for me! Frequently, while you were describing glimpses of your childhood, I was having flashes from *my* past that dredged up all the old feelings of guilt and anger from my youth. It's not fair, Richard . . . it's just not *fair!*"

By this time I was sitting next to her on the sofa, and even though my efforts seemed futile, I *was* able to take her into my arms and hold her quivering body next to mine. In the midst of her distress and tears, Maria finally posed a penetrating question. "Richard," she pleaded, "it seems that many times you've found in your old chest solutions to problems facing you and the kids. Isn't there anything in here for *me*?!"

Wanting the answer to be "yes," I reached over and lifted the lid of the box. While anxiously peering down inside, I said a silent prayer, asking Heavenly Father to guide my thoughts so that I might be able to help Maria. Knowing that the only memento we hadn't already used was an olive branch, I glanced at it but nothing seemed to be there that would help us. Puzzled, I searched inside the chest. Astonished, I noticed a slight separation between the lid and the piece of wood that held it together. Suddenly I had a vague memory about a hidden compartment inside. Working my hands over the wood, I was soon able to open what I now remembered as my "hiding place." And as I did, out tumbled a previously forgotten memento from my youth.

Rolled and tied in a blue silk ribbon was my Primary graduation certificate. Snuggling even closer to Maria, while untying the ribbon, I unrolled it until our eyes fell upon two signatures--one was of Sister Mary Newren, the Primary president at the time of my graduation, and the other was of Bishop Charles Pickett. Bishop Pickett interviewed me for Primary graduation and ordination into the Aaronic Priesthood. Turning the certificate toward Maria, I pointed to Bishop Pickett's signature and said, "Maybe there was something in that interview that could help us. . . ."

Bishop Pickett had been my bishop for over a decade. In fact, he was still serving when I was called on my mission. So, it didn't surprise me that his voice and mannerisms were easy to recall. That familiarity, however, did not explain the clarity of the scene that came into view as I described my Primary graduation interview. By now both Maria and I had stopped trying to explain how the treasure box had such an influence on us. We just went with the flow of the experience. Although the vivid recollection lasted only a brief few moments, we became so involved in the incident that it was almost as if Bishop Pickett were present and speaking to us now.

"As you know, Ricky," he began, looking right at me, "this is an important time of your life. You are now leaving Primary, and although this part of your childhood has passed, it will be forever buried in your memory. Some of these memories will be right below the surface and easy to dig up, while others will be buried much deeper. Nevertheless, everything in your past is located somewhere inside your mind."

Seeing that he had my total attention, he continued. "Ricky, you are now going to have your very first personal worthiness interview. During this time we will talk about events of your life, to make sure that you are worthy to hold the Aaronic priesthood. It is so important that you are completely honest in these interviews, Ricky."

His look was somehow both firm and gentle. He was a "no nonsense" sort of bishop, but the kind who could also have fun. But he knew when to be serious, and I could tell that this was one of those times. Nevertheless, I was struggling to understand the relationship between my "buried memories" and being honest in answering his questions. I guess he could see that I wasn't quite clear on the concept because he asked if *I* had any questions.

Clearing my throat, I swallowed one more time, then said, "Well, Bishop, I wonder why the emphasis on being very honest when we can just bury our past in our memories and forget it."

"That's a good question, Ricky," he rejoined in a considerate tone. "I guess the simple answer is that *buried* memories do not mean totally forgotten memories. They aren't completely forgotten by us, nor are they forgotten by our Heavenly Father. It's like this . . . your mind can either be a treasure chest or a garbage can. It's up to you; will you store buried treasure or buried trash?"

Now, I'll admit that what he was saying was starting to make sense to me. In addition, it didn't hurt that Uncle ValGene had made me a treasure chest and not a garbage can. Furthermore, I had learned long ago to put only special things inside it. So at least I understood the part about keeping buried treasures stored in my memory.

But Bishop Pickett didn't stop there. "Ricky," he continued, "everyone makes mistakes. But, if they don't repent of their misdeeds, the memory of what they've done can haunt them for a long time. Not repenting is like burying trash and using our mind as a garbage can instead of a treasure chest. That's why it's so important for you to be honest in your interviews. There are some things that Heavenly Father asks you to discuss with your bishop before you can be completely forgiven."

I really liked the fact that Bishop Pickett had moved his chair around in front of the desk and was not sitting far away. It made me more comfortable when I asked, "Bishop, in Primary we learned that when we repent, our lives--no matter how wrinkled they have become--are like a clean sheet of paper. Is that what you're saying?"

"Yes . . . but also a little bit more. You see, because of our Savior's sufferings in Gethsemane, it is possible to start over again. But repentance sometimes includes more than just confessing to Heavenly Father and the bishop, then changing what we have been doing."

Well, I knew about Gethsemane because of the olive branch from the Holy Land Sister Crowley had given me when she gave a lesson on forgiveness. If fact, I had saved that olive branch and put it in my special box. But I did wonder what else was necessary besides talking to Heavenly Father and the bishop. The conversation didn't go that way, though, because Bishop Pickett then began to talk about the priesthood, and about my worthiness to become a deacon. I got so excited about the thought of passing the sacrament that I just forgot to ask the question, and before I knew it the interview was over.

Just as quickly as this scene faded from view, Maria and I were back in the study. She was the first to speak. "Well, Richard," she sighed, wiping the steady flow of tears from her cheeks, "I'll never understand how the connection with your memory takes place, so I guess I'll just accept it. Nevertheless, I think the incident you've just related was for *me*. Bishop Pickett was right. I have a *lot* of trash and anger buried that needs to be thrown out. What was also clear to me was that I need to talk with my bishop again, only this time it's *you*. Do you think we could do that together somehow--soon?"

"Of course, " I returned, my relief visible. "I think if we work at this, we can do just fine. Let's get the kids off to bed, then drive over to the chapel. I think it might work better if we were in the bishop's office. What do you think?"

"I'd like that," Maria sniffed, smiling for the first time, and left to prepare dinner. And I began to reminisce. . . .

I remember that Maria and I first met when I was a student at a small college in Cedar City, Utah. As we became acquainted, I learned that her parents were originally active members of the Church, married in the Salt Lake Temple. Maria was born in Salt Lake City, and in her early years, attended Primary and all her other meetings; she was baptized by her father at the age of eight.

Maria seemed to recall her early childhood as a very happy one. Then things suddenly changed. It was shortly after her baptism that her father left home and never returned. Without an explanation, it took her a while to understand that her parents were divorced, and that her father was simply not interested in her *or* her mother. Because of this rejection, she remembered being very angry at her father during her teen years. She also had clear memories of her mother simply wilting away. In fact, not long after Maria's eighteenth birthday, her mother died. The official cause of death was cancer, but Maria was certain that she died of a broken heart. It was during the summer following her high school graduation that Maria buried her mother, as well as most of what she called her "painful" youth.

She recalled the months that followed as being very empty, almost as though she were existing in a void. Deep within her heart, she felt increasingly bitter. Sometimes these feelings of anger were even directed toward Heavenly Father. After all, she had already lost her father, so why hadn't the Lord saved her mother? More frequently, however, she was bitterly angry with her *earthly* father. Although she had neither seen nor spoken to him in many, many years, she blamed him for the misery she and her mother suffered after he abandoned them. She was certain that if he hadn't left them, her mother would still be alive.

For almost two years following her mother's death, Maria stayed away from Church. No entreaties from leaders helped. In fact, she deliberately moved to an apartment in a different part of town so that she couldn't be easily tracked.

During this time, she fell into serious transgression. Tragically, alcohol, drugs, and sexual activity filled her spare time. Although she experienced a hollow emptiness during this period, she had also found a group of friends who seemed to love and accept her as she was. At the time, she could ask for no more.

Maria often told me that she was rescued by an angel. She was certain that she never would have recovered, except for the unexpected appearance of a very special person. It was a little more than two years after her mother's death that Maria's paternal grandmother, Grandma Tierlink--or Momma T, as she was affectionately known--showed up at Maria's apartment.

I have always been deeply grateful that Momma T had stayed in touch with Maria after her father left. In fact, no birthday or special occasion ever passed in Maria's life without this wonderful grandmother acknowledging the event. For example, she drove all the way from Cedar City to Salt Lake City to attend Maria's high school graduation. She then sat proudly in the audience--next to Maria's mother--while Maria received her diploma. In short, Maria knew that her father's mother loved her. Momma T had proven that time and time again.

So, on one cold and wintry day, when Momma T showed up at her apartment, Maria was neither surprised nor angry. To the contrary, she was relieved. After a brief discussion, her grandmother offered to take her home to Cedar City, and Maria went without resistance. This devoted and caring matriarch had planned ahead. Knowing that Maria had relatively good grades in high school, Momma T arranged for Maria to start her freshman year that very month at the College of Southern Utah. Then, with the continual support of a loving grandmother, Maria rapidly regained her relationship with the Savior.

During this time, Maria met with a campus ward bishop who lovingly assisted her through the seldom-traveled road of repentance. Finally, two years later, and filled with the power of God, she was called to serve a full-time mission in France. There she spent 18 months teaching and internalizing Christ's gospel. At the conclusion of her mission, Maria returned to school where she became very active in her campus ward and the Institute of Religion.

And that was where we met--over cookies and punch following an Institute fireside. She often reminds me that, as a faithful returned missionary, I brought additional stability into her life. Within six months we were married--sealed for time and all eternity in the historic St. George Temple.

Within the first year of our marriage, Maria finished school. In fact, she graduated just days before the birth of our first child, Walter. Two years later I also graduated, and the three of us bade an emotional farewell to Momma T and moved to Provo so that I could pursue a Master's degree in education at Brigham Young University.

While in Provo, I studied hard and was fortunate to graduate with honors. Following graduation, I was accepted into a doctoral program at Columbia University. I had wanted to go east because I had served my mission in western New York state, and I felt a strong yearning to return there. So, with our station wagon filled with our belongings, we loaded our two children into our car and began our trek east across the plains. After several even more challenging years, I finished my studies, and we moved to Mendon.

To the present, our family of five has provided Maria with a wonderful source of fulfillment, although she has occasionally suggested that sometimes it is *too* full. From all outward appearances, however, we are viewed as a stable and faithful Latter-day Saint family. I'm sure that's why it seemed reasonable for our former bishop, in New York City, to call Maria to serve as Relief Society president. I know that I am biased, but Maria truly was a wonderful leader and servant to the members there. I heard countless comments about her sensitivity to the needs of the sisters and their families. She demonstrated a special affinity toward single sisters, and by experience, she understood what they were feeling in times of distress and loneliness.

With this kind of caring and sensitivity, one might assume that Maria had had no problems overcoming the abuse of abandonment and the effects of her sins. Even so, I now understood that such was not the case. Over the years, she had expressed some nagging concerns about her earlier life. Still, until the past few months I had no idea of the *depth* of these feelings.

These were my thoughts as I accompanied Maria to the chapel. Within minutes, we were comfortably seated in the office. Then, at Maria's request, we began her "interview" in prayer. As the prayer ended, we both arose, embraced with gentle emotion, then sat back down. As I had expected, Maria was very open as she briefly recounted details of her early life. I knew most of it already, of course, but she wanted to put our discussion in the context of the origin of her feelings.

Although I knew much about Maria's early life, I was shocked to discover the depth of her unresolved anger as she again recited the troubled story of her youth. As she unburdened her heart, for the very first time I began to understand why she had become increasingly *short* with us, and why she had shut the children out of any discussion of her childhood. It was simply too painful for her to talk about--with *anyone*, let alone our children. However, they were old enough now that it was becoming impossible to maintain the facade and keep her emotions in check.

As Maria continued, it became apparent that, in spite of the long hours she had spent with her campus ward bishop many years earlier, she still carried significant guilt for transgressions experienced during her years of rebellion and inactivity. While her years of Church service, a strong marriage, and reasonably responsible children had given her consolation, they had not laid to rest her fears and anger regarding all that had happened to her.

As she continued to share her experiences, she openly related her initial disclosures with her former bishop at college. It was clear that she had thoroughly confessed and repented of her misdeeds. In fact, her bishop had said as much. As she now related to me, he was certain she had done everything necessary to obtain forgiveness from her Heavenly Father.

With that sense of assurance, I asked, "Maria, if you were to choose a scripture that best describes your desired relationship with the Lord, what scripture would you choose?"

Replying slowly, but without hesitation, she said, "I would pick my favorite repentance scripture, Jeremiah 3:15. It says, 'Though your sins be as scarlet, they shall be white as snow.' *But,* Richard," she added earnestly, while leaning forward, "I know that reference by heart. Intellectually, I know the intent of that scripture and others such as, 'I the Lord will remember [your sins] no more.' I haven't been able to completely *internalize* the Lord's forgiveness . . . or to forgive *myself.*"

"Or to let your anger go by forgiving your father. . . ."

My words hit bedrock, and I could see that Maria now understood what I was saying. "Oh, Richard," she continued quickly, "I've been so out of sorts, and I know I've hurt you and the kids. I haven't wanted to, it's just that--"

"It's just that anger *always generalizes*, Maria, and now you will be able to expel it from your heart. I'm so sorry for what you've being going through. . . ."

"Does that mean you forgive me?"

Maria's words hit me like a brick! Forgive *her?!* I had never thought of it like that. Still, seizing the moment, I assured her that I had . . . if she had likewise forgiven *me* for the times I had been short with her.

An hour earlier, prior to our leaving the house, I had felt impressed to bring along the olive branch from my treasure box. I had wrapped it in soft tissue paper to protect it. Sensing that the time was right to reveal it, I pulled it from my coat pocket, unwrapped it, then told Maria about it. We agreed that it made sense that memories of an olive branch, the symbol of peace--especially one from the Holy Land-- might help both of us.

I began by relating in detail how, many years earlier, my Primary teacher gave a wonderful lesson about her visit to the Holy Land. I explained to Maria that at the conclusion of Sister Crowley's lesson, she gave each of us an olive branch that she had brought from Jerusalem. She had explained in depth how her visit had given her new insights into the Savior's life and exactly what He had done for us.

As I finished relating this incident, we both agreed that while it was an interesting remembrance--and perhaps a symbol of the atonement--we didn't see a direct relationship to Maria's feelings of guilt and unresolved anger. As we talked for the next two hours, it became clear that Maria had spent great effort over a considerable period of time trying to get over her fears of unworthiness. Still, she had simply not been successful. Even though I gave her the assurance of forgiveness I felt from the Lord, I honestly didn't feel like we made much progress.

We returned home tired and a little disheartened. As we walked in the house, I continued on up to my study so that I could return the olive branch to its place in the chest. I was perplexed to think that the olive branch story seemed to have no application. It was the first time an item from the box had failed to get to the bottom of things after I had felt impressed to use it.

Little did either of us know, as we had our prayers and slipped into bed that night, that this was only the beginning of our relationship with the small, twisted branch.

26

The Olive Branch

One Sunday afternoon, not long after our initial visit, Maria told me of an exciting phone call she had received just moments earlier. Momma T had called and announced that for our wedding anniversary she wanted to send us on a trip to the Holy Land. Discussing this generous offer over lunch, we decided to go. Truly, it seemed like a once-in-a-lifetime opportunity.

Later in the evening, Maria called her grandmother and gratefully accepted her generous offer. Though Maria's grandmother was in her early eighties, she was in excellent health. She insisted that we do it this way: she would pay for the children's flight to Utah so they could stay with her. We would fly out there to retrieve them, and to debrief *her,* upon our return.

In preparing for our trip, I suggested to Maria that we take the olive branch from the treasure box with us. This suggestion seemed strangely sensible to both of us, so we carefully packed it in one of the smaller suitcases.

Before long, Maria and I were soaring over the vast

Atlantic Ocean, on our way to London, then Cairo. Because were with an organized tour, we began in Egypt, where Joseph and Mary fled following the threats of Herod the Great. This was a poignant starting point, which only heightened the anticipation of entering the Holy Land a few days later.

Before arriving in Jerusalem, our tour stopped at Mount Sinai where we were reminded of the old Law that was ultimately fulfilled by Christ. It was also at Sinai that I became even more aware of the extent of the burden Maria was carrying. Although enjoying the trip, she was still feeling the weight of guilt. Just before we left the top of the mountain, I found a quiet, private place behind some rocks and gave Maria a blessing. Her spirits seemed to lift as we walked down the mountain and continued our trip.

We went into Israel by way of Jordan. Entering the fertile lands of Israel was indeed like entering the Promised Land, and we could only compare our feelings with those of the children of Israel as they concluded their forty years in the wilderness.

Once in Israel, where we were to spend the next ten days, we traveled in an air-conditioned bus with a Jewish guide named Abraham, a native of Israel. Not long after getting acquainted with him, we opened the suitcase that contained the olive branch and showed it to him. He told us that such a branch was a "good" symbol of Israel, where olive trees were plentiful. He said he would even point some out along the way.

One of the most inspirational moments of the trip took place near the northern Sea of Galilee, where Christ gave the Sermon on the Mount. While grouped together in the beautiful garden at the top of this mount, Abraham shared portions of that marvelous discourse given by the Master. As he stood in the shade of an old olive tree, we listened carefully and understood more clearly than ever before the meaning of the Savior's words. I was particularly impressed with the principles Christ taught concerning compassion, caring, and forgiving, as expressed by this Jewish guide, who seemed to really *believe* what he was telling us.

The following morning, as we were driving toward Jerusalem, Abraham pointed out the valley where Christ supposedly taught the rich young ruler. For a few moments the bus stopped near a large and very old olive tree. There Abraham reminded us that the young man told the Master that he had obeyed all the basic commandments since his youth. In response, Christ had said, "One thing thou lackest." Then, as Abraham eloquently expressed, Jesus challenged this young man to sell all of his earthly goods, give them to the poor, and follow Him.

While Abraham was relating this story, Maria and I looked at each other with an almost sardonic smile. We acknowledged that we possessed so little of the world's goods that the poor wouldn't get much if we followed that advice. In fact, we laughed, if everyone in the United States did *that*, our family would end up getting the best of it!

While we continued our journey up into Jerusalem, Abraham walked back in the bus to where Maria and I were sitting. He was carrying a paper cup with water in it. At first we thought he was bringing us a drink from his water bottle; for in this hot, arid country, water was often in short supply, so all the tour buses carried plenty. But this was not Abraham's purpose. Rather, he asked Maria if he could see her olive branch.

To our surprise, he poured several drops of water onto the bark and began to rub it gently into the wood. As he did this, he explained that there was more than one type of olive tree. One was less common, he added, because it was so difficult to cultivate. After softening the bark, he rubbed his fingernail vigorously on the surface. Then, after he had broken through the bark, he held the branch up toward us and asked us to smell it. Unexpectedly, we detected a rich, pungent lemon smell.

"Last night," he began in near perfect English, "it occurred to me that you might have a branch from the lemon olive tree. For some reason, these trees emit a lemon-like odor from their bark. The taste of the bark is very bitter, but the fruit of the lemon olive tree is most prized of all. This fruit is sweeter to the taste than any other olive, and the oil extracted from these olives produces the purest of all olive oil. While it is true that the olive tree is generally found throughout Israel, the lemon olive tree is most rare. It takes much care to grow lemon olive trees, and in spite of the high value of the fruit, most olive growers don't have the patience to produce the trees."

Seeing he had captured our attention, he continued. "You have been given a branch from a lemon olive tree. It is possible that we have not been near one so far, as they rarely grow in the wild. However, we'll be stopping by one later today, and I'll point it out to you."

For a while we were intrigued by the thought that our branch was from a *lemon* olive tree. As the day wore on, however, we became caught up in the new sites and sounds of old Jerusalem. Toward the end of the afternoon, the bus pulled to a stop in front of the Garden of Gethsemane.

I'll admit that the thought of being on this hallowed hillside brought a sense of almost overwhelming reverence to both Maria and me. We were talking about these feelings as we stepped off the bus, when suddenly Abraham interrupted our discussion with a request that we follow him. As we walked up the road and into the garden, I felt a reverence I could not explain. Taking Abraham's lead, we walked along a narrow path toward the back of the garden. He then directed us toward a large, gnarled tree. Quietly, he scratched the bark of the tree and immediately the aroma of lemon filled the air. It was a much stronger smell than from our little branch. Abraham then left us alone while he walked back along the path toward the others on the tour.

"Richard," Maria whispered, "isn't it marvelous that in Gethsemane we find a living reminder of the sacred event that occurred here so long ago."

Frankly, I hadn't really thought about it that deeply. So,

in my typically obtuse manner, I asked, "What to do you mean?"

"Well," she explained patiently, "from a most bitter source comes the purest and sweetest fruit of all olive trees. From the most bitter of moments in all of history have come the sweetest gifts from the Son of God."

"That's a marvelous insight," I replied honestly, "but I'm still wondering what this olive branch has to do with helping you resolve your standing with the Lord."

"Richard," she replied emphatically, "I think it is clear that we are here in this sacred place to help me find my way back to Him. Maybe it would be good if I had a few minutes to myself. Would you mind?"

Respecting her privacy, and wanting a moment to myself for my _own_ prayer, I squeezed her hand then silently walked away.

Before long, we were back on the bus, marveling at the most singular moment of our tour. We then headed south, inching our way toward the village of Bethlehem. I hadn't realized it was part of the West Bank until that moment, and I instantly ached because of the animosity that was apparent between the Israelis and the Palestinians.

We saw other sites, as well, and were continually humbled at the privilege of being where Christ's mortal ministry had taken place so long ago. Nothing, however, compared to being in the Garden of Gethsemane.

That night, as we returned to our hotel, Maria invited me to read her journal entry recorded earlier while on the bus. Sitting in a chair next to an open window, I began to read:

October 12th:

> Today I was able to go off by myself and ponder the meaning of what had happened in the sacred Garden of Gethsemane. During this peaceful time, I reflected upon the sins of my past. As these transgressions passed before my mind, I remembered

that this was the place where Christ suffered most intensely for *all* of my personal sins. Even my most grievous transgressions had been balanced here.

Leaving Richard, I found a secluded spot at the end of the lower walkway. Then kneeling on that sandy soil, I began to ponder the suffering Savior, my Redeemer, as He had knelt on this same soil. Immediately and without forethought, I began to review what I knew about the magnitude of His suffering. The mixture of remembering and actually being here caused a wave of gratitude to sweep over my entire frame. This overwhelming feeling of appreciation triggered my emotions, causing tears to stream down my checks. While kneeling there, I cried out, "My Lord, if you paid for my transgressions so many years ago, then *why* do I have no peace? I just don't understand. . . ."

Slowly, from deep inside, a warm sensation began until it grew larger and larger. It continued growing until I thought I was going to be consumed by it. Just at that instant, a soft and tender voice came into my mind. The voice seemed to say, *One thing thou lackest. . . .*

Immediately, I thought of our financial condition, and again I whispered, "But, we have so little of things of the world, I have nothing to give. Nevertheless, whatever you require, I will give."

Then with a power I can't explain, the voice came back into my mind and said, *My daughter, you must give away **all** of your sins. During this trip, you have been reminded of what you lack. Think back upon what you heard in the shade of the olive tree while in my land, and you will know what you must give.*

Gradually the warm sensation subsided. Wiping the tears from my face, I arose from my knees and began to walk back up the path. And as I walked, I pondered the meaning of what had just transpired. I mentally reviewed our journey and remembered Abraham's discussion about the Sermon on the Mount. Somehow I knew that the requirement would be found in the words of the Master, as contained within this timeless sermon. I was carrying my scriptures with me, so quickly I opened the New Testament to Matthew chapter five. As I glanced through the verses, I finally reached verses twenty-three and twenty-four, which read:

> *Therefore, if thou bring thy gift to the altar, and there rememberest that thy brother hath ought against thee; Leave there thy gift before the altar, and go thy way; first be reconciled to thy brother, and then come and offer thy gift.*

It was at that moment that I knew--DADDY! My *father* was the answer to my quest, and somehow--somewhere--I knew that I must find him.

Rushing up the path, I was almost out of breath when I rounded a turn and ran directly into Richard's arms. Tears flowed as I related my experience, and all the while he remained silent. What I didn't know at that time was that Richard--on his own--had been kneeling beneath an ancient olive tree in another part of the garden, praying that I would at long last receive the answer to my prayer.

Silently, and arm in arm, we exited the garden and returned to our tour bus. As we slowly left the hill and drove alongside the Brook Kidron, I knew that the Holy Spirit would guide me to my daddy--to him and to peace!

27

*T*hey Shall Be

White As Snow

Throughout our flight back to the states, Maria and I talked about what we had to do next. She was certain, however, that there were some things she was going to have to face alone and resolve without me. Because we had left the kids at Momma T's, we would need to return to Utah to get them. Maria had no idea where her father lived, or even if he were *alive*, but she knew that Momma T would know. After all, he *was* her son, and surely he would not have deserted her, too.

By the time we arrived back in Cedar City, five days had passed since Maria's experience in the Garden of Gethsemane. Needless to say, her anxiety about finding and meeting with her father was at a fever pitch. She held back many of these emotions, however, until we had spent time with the kids. Finally, when she couldn't stand it any longer, she sent them into the family room, explaining that we needed to talk with Momma T alone.

She then led Momma T and me into the privacy of the living room. Sensing her anxiety, we quietly followed her.

Once in the room, while taking Maria's hand in hers, Momma T asked, "What's the matter, dear?" The familiarity of those soft and caring hands seemed to cause Maria's anxiety to drain away, and her entire frame appeared to sigh in relief.

"Momma T," she stammered, her voice quivering, "I must find *Daddy*! As you know, I haven't seen him or spoken to him in over 10 *years*! I'm ashamed to admit this, Momma T, but he did call me twice after Mother passed away."

"Go on, Dearie," Momma T encouraged tenderly.

"The first time I spoke with him was a few days before Richard and I were married. He called, identified himself, and asked if he might attend the wedding. By suggesting that he was *able* to attend, I think he was attempting to tell me of his personal worthiness, that he had put his life together. But, without even giving him a chance to finish his explanation, I told him absolutely not. I added that I thought it was an absurd and selfish request, and that having him there would spoil everything. 'After all,' I had self-righteously exclaimed, 'it's *my* day, not *yours*.' In no uncertain terms, Mamma T, I *demanded* that he never call again!"

Looking into Momma T's eyes, I could sense the pain she felt. I wanted to respond to her, but instead I listened as Maria continued. "Momma T, Daddy's second call came about a decade ago. Luke had just been born, and Daddy called the Sunday before the blessing. He asked to participate in this priesthood ordinance. My response was as cold as before the wedding, Momma T. I told him it was a pointless exercise to try to reconcile with me. No matter what he did, I would never meet with him or initiate a conversation with him. Again, I didn't let him explain, nor did I consider that he was trying to tell me that he had found his way back."

Maria suddenly stopped speaking. After several seconds her eyes lit up, and she exclaimed, "It just dawned on me,

Momma T, *how* Daddy knew when to make those two calls."

"Yes, dear," Momma T sighed, smiling, "now you know. I'm afraid I'm the culprit. But please don't fault me for it. After all, he *is* my son."

"And *my* father, Momma T. And, no, I don't fault you at all. If anything, knowing this just makes me love you more. But . . . now I must find him . . . that is . . . if he's still--"

"*Alive?!* Yes, honey, he is alive, and I suspect that more than anything else in the world, he would also like to speak with you."

At that instant, a rush of emotions swept over Maria with such force that she could hardly breathe. After taking time to allow her tears to subside, she choked, "I just realized I just envisioned you kneeling on this old, creaking floor. I'm sure it wasn't a single prayer, but many prayers spoken by you, year-after-year-after-year. Momma T, I can just hear your pleading voice seeking the Lord's help to reunite your two loved ones--both once lost, and now reconciled to Him, but not to each other."

Gently, and without any hint of criticism, Momma T replied, "You are right, my dear, and as you may remember, I had many conversations with you, suggesting as tactfully as I could that you find your father. I'm glad I didn't give up, but I couldn't just leave it to luck or good fortune. I have spent a few nights deepening the furrows in the old pine boards by the side of my bed, talking with Heavenly Father about helping me."

"Thank you so much, Momma T. I think it's now time, and I need to find him. I am sure you know where he is, so will you help me?"

Without reply, Momma T pulled Maria's face down toward her. Burying her head in Maria's shoulder, Momma T began to sob quietly, "Oh, sweetheart, it has finally *happened!* The day has finally arrived!"

Lifting her head and looking into Maria's eyes, Momma T spoke with continued emotion. "Your father is living in

Salt Lake City, and of course, I know how to find him."
Getting up, she walked across the room and opened the
drawer of a side table. She came back holding a small white
business card in her hand which she gave directly to her
granddaughter.

Upon examining it, Maria noted that the card was both
elegant and understated. Engraved on it was simply his
name, his address, and his phone home number in Salt Lake
City. It was time, and from the look in Maria's eyes, I could
tell that nothing would keep her from her rendevous with
destiny--destiny and peace.

28

Sharing Feelings

That night, long after the rest of us had retired, Maria wrote her impressions to her father in a letter she wanted to give to him. Because Maria hadn't wanted her first contact with her father to be a phone call, Momma T placed the call and arranged for Maria and her father to meet the following afternoon.

Early the next morning, we said our goodbyes to Maria's grandmother, then drove north to Salt Lake City. The four-hour drive was one filled with sweet conversation. Maria recalled that over the years I had made every effort to be patient with her, and even though I knew the anguish her father had caused her, I never pressed her to reconcile with him. When I did encourage her to locate him, she was so adamantly opposed that I knew things would have to find their own time and place. In all of this I decided to simply be supportive and allow the Lord to do the rest.

As we drove north on I-15, Maria became aware of the other "player" in this drama. She knew her father must also be reliving *his* fears, and she knew his anxiety would at least match hers as he awaited their arrival. In the quiet moments of the trip, she was filled with apprehension as she tried to imagine seeing this man for whom she had harbored a lifetime of ugly feelings.

Finally, we arrived in Salt Lake City. Following Momma T's carefully sketched map, we immediately made our way to the Holladay area, where Maria's father and his wife Karen were living. Strangely, their home was not at all what either Maria *or* I had pictured. Somehow in the past, Maria had mentally and verbally demonized this man, envisioning him as being almost subhuman. She had always pictured him as a derelict, a broken person who was suffering a wasted life. Maria's thoughts had even wandered so far as to think that perhaps he was a homeless person on the streets of some large city. But this home, located beneath the spectacular Wasatch Mountains, was very attractive. The neighborhood was anything but run-down, and the flower-filled yard was almost perfectly manicured.

As we pulled up in front of the house, Maria whispered that her heart had almost stopped beating. I suggested that I drive around with the kids and return in about two hours. Suddenly, Maria said felt like she was re-living her first day at kindergarten, when her mother finally left her alone at the door of the school. Still, she felt my suggestion was right, although *she did* ask me to wait long enough for her to get safely inside.

Clutching her purse in one hand and the envelope containing her letter in the other, she somehow made her way to the front door. My heart was literally racing as I watched her ring the bell. After all, she was about to face the man she had hated for over thirty years.

The door swung open, and what Maria saw in front of her was not at all what she expected. There stood a handsome gentleman in his mid-sixties. His was not a face that carried the scars of years of unrighteous living, pocked with the ravages of sin. Rather, it was a kind face, the face of her children's grandfather. His well-groomed, white hair framed the countenance of one who had experienced years of giving--years full of righteous living and countless acts of kindness.

I can only describe with intimate details the events that followed because of Maria's telling the story to us several time during the next few days. As Maria's father took her hands in his, she immediately recognized those hands. To Maria, they felt like her grandmother's hands. When he spoke, she could hear in his voice the kindness of his mother--that wonderful woman who had worked a lifetime for this moment.

"Maria," he asked at last, "is it really *you?!*"

"*Daddy?!!*"

Maria had not spoken that name for many, many years, yet somehow it came out in a burst. She had carefully protected the name over her lifetime, until it had become almost a sacred title--a title symbolic of her early memories of her father. To Maria, it was a title that had to be earned--earned by a lifetime of love. In fact, she had not used it to refer to this man since he left her and her mother. Now, however, it seemed *so* good to Maria to say the word and to accept its meaning in her heart.

After the two greeted, and not knowing exactly what else to say, Maria waved goodby to the rest of us, as we had remained in the car. As her father invited her inside, she indicated that she had a letter for him. Not surprisingly, Maria's father also had a letter for *her*, parts of which had been written some time earlier. In fact, he told Maria that he had written several versions of his letter along the way, each one updated when it appeared that she might allow him to reenter her life.

So that the two might read their letters more comfortably, Maria's father suggested they retire to his study. For Maria, the walk through the entryway, then across the living room into the back of the house, was very revealing. On one of the walls in the living room were photographs that spread almost from floor to ceiling. They were mostly group pictures of a man, clearly her father, standing near a woman somewhat younger than he. The pictures were arranged chronologically, so it was easy to follow their history. The first was of the two of them alone, then the two of them in a group with the woman dressed in a wedding dress outside the St. George Temple. Next was the two of them with a child. Then another and another until six children surrounded them. Next came a wedding picture, then two more, and finally there were large group photos, including grandchildren. Maria didn't stop to count how many grandchildren she observed, but there *were* many.

They then came to a second grouping of pictures only slightly separated from the first group. The first was of a couple in their early twenties. It had been taken outside of the Salt Lake Temple. Maria instantly recognized the woman as her mother. Next to that picture was one of a small smiling child, and then several snapshots of three people--father, mother and daughter. To the right of those portraits, yet still included as part of the larger family group, was a photograph of another wedding. Maria's heart seemed to leap into her throat as she realized that it was of her and Richard at the St. George Temple. Almost unable to breathe, she realized that she was looking at many portraits of the two of them with their children. This section was current and up to date. These were duplicates of some of the pictures she had sent to Momma T, and now she understood. . . .

While Maria examined each of the portraits along the wall, her father spoke very little. He just held her hand and occasionally introduced her to some of his other children and grandchildren. Sensing what had taken place inside Maria's heart, he finally said, "Maria, this is your sister, Connie. This is your brother, Ralph. . . ."

As they arrived at the section of Maria's family, he added, "Your grandmother kept me up to date."

Other than those comments, Maria's father didn't speak. Rather, he sensed the wisdom of letting it all settle in

139

slowly. He merely allowed her to linger as she absorbed what she was seeing. Maria sensed that he wanted her to realize that she had always been part of something larger than she had known.

As father and daughter continued on through the house, Maria became keenly aware of the unusually fine furnishings. It was apparent to her that this was a man of some wealth. It wasn't showy, however, but was decorated tastefully.

They finally arrived at the study and settled comfortably together on a leather sofa. Maria silently handed her father her letter, and he in turn gave Maria his. As she opened it, she could see that although it was recently typed, it had been written over a period of many years--almost journal-like--with new paragraphs added as time and circumstances changed. From the date scrolled along the top, the original letter was written about the time she started attending college in Cedar City.

Maria could immediately sense that her father's letter was a treasure, written by a man who patiently sought reconciliation with a daughter he clearly loved. In it he gently and forgivingly wrote of his pain following the times Maria rejected his approaches. She learned that he had been the source of the anonymous scholarship given to her so many years ago. She had known that her high school grades were good enough to get her into college, but she had wondered how she had ever earned a full four-year tuition scholarship. At the time, Momma T had said only that she had arranged it. In the letter, Maria's father did not speak of his contribution proudly. He simply expressed appreciation that he had found a way to help.

Continuing to read, Maria found that the paragraphs in which her father talked about his leaving Maria and her mother were very brief. He had written that he had made a series of terrible mistakes. . .mistakes from which he did not recover until after her mother, his childhood sweetheart, had passed away. He talked about his own irreconcilable grief when she died. From the letter, Maria learned that it was during her funeral that he had come to his senses, recognizing that if he continued along his current path of destruction, he would perish and eternally forfeit everything. Subsequently, with Momma T's help, he put his own life back together. Apparently, she had brought him to the funeral, somehow balancing her time being with him while comforting Maria. Maria hadn't even noticed him there, and no doubt could not have handled any confrontation. Wisely, she considered, Momma T had kept them apart.

In the paragraphs that followed, Maria's father described other direct, but until now, unknown attempts to reconcile. He had even flown out to Rochester and had driven down to Mendon! However, he became so certain of another rejection that he flew back home after having driven only once by Maria's house.

The last few paragraphs, written the night before, were the sweetest of all. As Maria began to read them, she suddenly felt the pages being lifted from her hands. Turning to face her father, Maria was surprised to hear him say, "Honey, may I read this part of my letter to you? I've pictured this moment so many times, and I want you to *feel* my words as well as to hear them."

Allowing her mind to relax, Maria dropped her hands in her lap, and listened as he began:

"Dear Maria,

"I now know the way! This past month my wife, Karen, and I went on a two-week trip to Israel. It was the experience of a lifetime. The trip itself seemed to be a time of completion. Never have I understood the mission of the Master as I do now, after having walked where he walked. One experience, however, stands out among all the others.

"A moment of quiet and profound revelation came as we visited that hallowed garden where the God of

141

the universe bought us with his blood. While standing there contemplating the most significant event in history, the Lord showed me the way to personal reconciliation with you.

"I was on my knees in a quiet part of the garden. It was there that I cried out in my mind, *Dear Father, I am growing old. Is there not any hope that I can find peace with my beloved daughter during this life? Must I wait until death to finish the reconciliation with her, as well as with her mother? I know that the blood of thy Son has purchased my forgiveness, but I cannot find true peace until I hear words of acceptance from Maria, as well. If only in this life I could hear the voice of my sweet daughter telling me that all was well, I could go to my grave in peace. Please, oh, please, help me.*

"Maria, this was not an unfamiliar prayer to Heavenly Father. I have offered variations of it for many years. But there in Gethsemane I heard the answer I was seeking.

"In my mind, new thoughts came gently and slowly, teaching me the way. As I left the garden, I knew that the time of reconciliation was approaching, although I had something to do beforehand.

"On that day in Jerusalem, in that sacred garden, the Spirit taught me a great lesson. *William,* a voice softly called into my mind, *would that I could bring each of my children to this hallowed spot. Truly, each one who comes to me with a broken heart must walk the path of this garden, and become intimately acquainted with what transpired here. While not all can come here, Maria can. Go home and arrange a trip for her and Richard to come to this place. I will provide a way for them to be convinced of the trip's value. I will help her discover the most important trail in this garden. It is the path to complete love and peace.*

"My response, Maria, was one of reluctance as well as excitement. I knew the outcome was certain, but I didn't know how to make sure that you would come. Still, peace came to my mind as I could picture my mother calling you once again with another of her wonderful ideas.

"Then I asked, perhaps inappropriately, how He would soften your heart. He revealed to me your continuing turmoil about your own standing before him. I understood that He had patiently encouraged you to resolve your feelings of hostility toward me, but you could not. So, in a loving attempt to assist you--and consistent with his plan--He withheld from you a sense of complete reconciliation with Him.

"At that moment, in some miraculous way, I saw in my mind your visit to this holy place. I heard you cry out for peace. And I heard these words spoken in my mind. *One thing thou lackest, Maria. Go and become reconciled to thy father, and then return to the altar. THEN, AND ONLY THEN, if thy sins be as scarlet, they shall become as white as the driven snow.*

"While I am the cause of your pain, my daughter, know that I am ready to do my part in removing this thorn from your heart. Tomorrow we will finally be able to put this behind us and start anew.

"Your loving and anxious father"

Concluding the final sentence of his letter, Maria's father looked up for the first time since beginning to read. Their eyes then met--as father and daughter--for the first time in almost 35 years.

After several moments in each other's arms, the two finally drew back and began to talk. The words each spoke were sweet, and Maria especially appreciated his response to *her* letter. She had offered forgiveness for anything she had suffered because of his earlier mistakes. Maria then told

143

her father that when she had written the letter, she had known nothing of his current life, or of his standing before the Lord. Nor did she know how the trip to Gethsemane had really been arranged. As she then expressed, she only knew that she accepted him unconditionally as her father and as the grandfather of her children.

"Daddy," she finally paused, while glancing down at her own letter to her father. It lay in his lap, and was turned to the page that she treasured most. "I'm not able to read what I next said to you, so why don't I just look over your shoulder while you read it to yourself. I just wrote it last night, so you needn't read it out loud."

Squeezing her father's hand, she then looked over at her letter, and skimmed along the sentences while her father silently read each and every word:

Daddy, last week in the Garden of Gethsemane, in the midst of my continuing agony regarding the magnitude of my sins, I learned that it is impossible for one to attain complete reconciliation without possessing a Christ-like spirit of forgiveness.

And now, tomorrow, you will be holding this letter in your hand. I only hope you can forgive me for the feelings I have retained in my heart. This bitterness has robbed me of years that I could have spent with you in my life. While you have repeatedly held out the olive branch, I have just as often rejected it.

From this day forward, you shall be the grandfather of my children. And you shall be my "daddy" for as long as the eternities. What was once bitter, has now become sweet. How appropriate and ironic it is that only __through__ you can I find peace.

Now I know assuredly that though my sins be as scarlet, on the morrow at your home they will become as white as the driven snow.

All my love and devotion, Maria

After thirty more minutes of visiting and catching up, the phone rang. Maria's father picked it up, listened, and then handed it to her. That was my call, as I had promised, two hours after we dropped her off.

"I'm just a couple of blocks away, honey," I began. "But I've got a surprise sitting next to me, and I think you'll like it."

"*Another* surprise? I'm not sure I can handle much more, Richard!"

"This one you can just hug. It's Momma T. Last night, while you were writing your letter to your dad, she and I arranged for her to leave Cedar City right after we did, on the mighty Greyhound. She said we needed the time to be alone with the kids, but I think she thought a bus ride would be more comfortable."

"What you mean is that *she* needed to be alone *without* the kids!"

"I think you're right, but we'll not ask." We laughed before Maria asked, "Why are we talking on the phone when you could just come on over? Something wonderful is happening and you all need to be a part of it."

Within minutes, Momma T, the kids, and I drove up in front of the house. Maria and her father were standing in the yard, waiting. Maria had just met Karen, her father's wife. In their first conversation, Maria somehow knew that this woman was the source of her father's energy and resolve. Maria also sensed that her children were gaining a set of grandparents that would forever change and bless their lives.

So it was that the last item in the treasure box, the branch from the lemon olive tree, came to impact my life, the lives of my family members, and those who loved us most. At first it was strange to me this last treasure seemed to direct us to the future, and not the past. But this was not exactly true. In actuality, this branch from the magical lemon olive tree was from my Primary past, given to me by a thoughtful teacher. This primary worker had likewise found reconciliation with her Heavenly Father at the foot of an old olive tree deep in the Garden of Gethsemane. Thus it can be seen that on that sacred hillside there is a crossroads of the past, present, and future that transcends anything known to mortal man. For there, somehow, the sins of all meet in infinite time, to be washed away in the sufferings of the Eternal God, before whom *all* things--past, present and future--are seen as one.

So it should surprise no one that I found much about my past and something about my future locked inside an old treasure box. Although it seemed that I had at last emptied my wondrous chest of its valuable contents, and that my world of old boxes was about to disappear, such was not the case. . . .

E*pilogue*

On a Tuesday afternoon, not long after our return from Utah and Israel, I was sitting upstairs in my den, gazing longingly at my old chest. I had just placed the olive branch back into its permanent place in the box, and was somewhat preoccupied when Maria walked into the room. I hadn't even noticed her until she interrupted me with an implied question.

"Richard, Richard . . . a penny for your thoughts."

Startled, I looked up at her and quickly reviewed what had so completely captured my attention. "I guess I was thinking about the magic of this wonderful old trunk. . . ."

"Uh-oh," she responded with mocked sarcasm. "What on earth is going to happen next?"

"Well, as usual, you've hit the nail on the head. Nothing's going to happen next. I've used this box up. There isn't an item left in it that we haven't talked about. So what am I to do for solutions to problems as they come up?"

Just then the phone rang. It was our ward Primary president who explained, "We've planned an outing to the

Hill Cumorah this afternoon, and one of our drivers canceled. We're leaving the chapel in fifteen minutes. Could you possibly drive a carload of ten-year-old girls?"

Forty-five minutes and many ten-year-old giggles later, I found myself at the top of the Hill Cumorah, about twenty feet below the angel Moroni statue. We all listened intently as one of the teachers presented a beautiful testimony of some of the miraculous events that took place there.

"Now, girls," she enthused, "it was somewhere near here that the Prophet Joseph Smith unearthed an ancient, stone treasure chest. Beneath the stone lid and inside the box was a sacred memento from the distant past. This discovery, of course, was the golden plates. Centuries later, this golden treasure was to provide answers to problems for literally millions of people. When we read from the translation of the gold plates placed in that box so many years ago, it is as if time stands still. We can literally see in our minds and feel in our hearts the events that transpired at that time. Isn't it wonderful that the Spirit of the Lord can transcend time and space and make those deeds of long ago become an active part of *our* lives?!"

In that instant, with a new and profound understanding, I was certain that I would never be without a treasure from an ancient, well-crafted box. *So I will be able to use Moroni's treasures,* I reasoned silently, *when I need to sort out issues that trouble either me or those I love.*

In my reverie, while listening to this inspired Primary teacher, I spoke softly to no one else but myself. "Well, Richard," I whispered wistfully out into the late afternoon breeze, "here you are, proving once again that all you *really* need to know you learned in Primary. . . ."

AUTHOR'S END NOTE

As we prepared to publish this book, we received several requests from friends of other faiths--asking us to rewrite the book through a more general Christian lens. This we have done, entitling the book, *ALL I REALLY NEED TO KNOW I LEARNED IN SUNDAY SCHOOL.* Therefore, if you know someone of another faith--and you feel the story merits mention-- perhaps you could refer this title to them. Both books are a precursor to a third volume we are presently writing, titled, *CONRAD'S LITTLE BOOK OF VIRTUES.* It is our hope to fill it full of valuable treasures.

Additionally, we created the metaphor of the *lemon* olive tree to heighten the pathos of the story. This comparison to the Savior's bitter cup seemed to give further depth to the story. However, we must be clear that such a tree does not exist.

Finally, we hope that you have enjoyed this journey of *discovery, recovery, and hope* as much as we have enjoyed writing it.